Holl House
22-7-82   12.95

D1187388

VANIER PUBLIC LIBRARY
BIBLIOTHÈQUE PUBLIQUE VANIER
300 avenue des Pères Blancs
300 White Fathers Avenue
Vanier (Ontario) K1L 7L5

BY THE SAME AUTHOR

For Young Readers

Akavak
The White Archer
Tikta'liktak
Eagle Mask
Wolf Run
Ghost Paddle
Songs of the Dream People:
Chants and Images from the Indians and Eskimos
of North America

Kiviok's Magic Journey: An Eskimo Legend
Frozen Fire: A Tale of Courage
River Runners: A Tale of Hardship and Bravery
Long Claws: An Arctic Adventure

For Adults

The White Dawn (a novel)
Ghost Fox (a novel)
Spirit Wrestler (a novel)
Eskimo Prints
Ojibway Summer

BLACK DIAMONDS
A SEARCH FOR ARCTIC TREASURE

BLACK DIAMONDS

A SEARCH FOR ARCTIC TREASURE

BY JAMES HOUSTON
DRAWINGS BY THE AUTHOR

McCLELLAND AND STEWART

Copyright © 1982 by James Houston

All rights reserved

The Canadian Publishers
McClelland and Stewart Limited
25 Hollinger Road
Toronto M4B 3G2

Canadian Cataloguing in Publication Data

Houston, James, 1921–
    Black diamonds

    Sequel to: Frozen fire.
    ISBN 0-7710-4247-7

    I. Title.

    PS8515.086B52   jC813′.54   C82-094078-X
    PZ7.H819B1

Published simultaneously in the United States by
Atheneum Publishers

Composition by American–Stratford Graphic Services, Inc.
Brattleboro, Vermont
Manufactured in the United States of America by
Fairfield Graphics
Fairfield, Pennsylvania
First Edition

To my mother,
who had love, energy
and good ideas.

Frozen Fire, the adventure that preceded this book, related some of the true events that occurred on Baffin Island when a concerned boy—with his Inuk friend—went in search of his father and was lost in the Canadian Arctic. Fighting both fierce animals and killing storms, he and his friend finally won their desperate struggle for survival. That book ended there.

In *Black Diamonds*, Matthew and Kayak journey even farther north and west. They travel to one of the most remote and mysterious islands in the world and match wits with violent weather and strange men in a series of daring adventures and discoveries as they search for Arctic treasure.

James Houston
Northwest Territories
Canada, 1981

1. FROBISHER BAY   2. INUKSHUKSHALIK

3. PRINCE CHARLES ISLAND

Contents

BLACK DIAMONDS

A SEARCH FOR ARCTIC TREASURE

I

GOLD FEVER

"GOLD!" MATT MORGAN'S FATHER SAID. "DON'T EVER mention gold to me again, or copper either. It was my rush to get rich on precious metals that got us into all that trouble. I'm finished trying to stake out any mineral claims. I tell you, Charlie, I'm through with all of that nonsense. I'm settling down. I'm going to teach geology right here on Baffin Island."

"Good thinking," said Charlie, an Australian helicopter pilot. "Teaching is a better way for you to make a living, and it saves wear and tear on poor *Waltzing Matilda,* too. Ask Kayak. He'll tell you that is so."

Kayak was fifteen years old. Like his friend, Matthew, his face was drawn and thin from the long trek they had recently made in search of Mr. Morgan, but he was still strong and sturdy. He had blue-black hair, square white teeth, dark eyes and a wide, handsome face that was deeply tanned. Kayak was the son of an Inuit hunter and had lived on Baffin Island all his life. Like the others, he was surprised and pleased to find himself alive, though hospitalized, after the terrible dangers he and Matthew had survived when they searched for Mr. Morgan and Charlie, whose helicopter, *Waltzing Matilda*, had been downed.

Kayak reached into the pocket of his hospital dressing gown and took something out. He looked first at tall, thin Charlie with his bright red hair, then at Mr. Morgan, a powerfully built man, who now lay in a hospital bed. Then he turned to Matthew, "Mattoosie," he said, pronouncing his name for Matt in the soft Inuktitut way, "I got something to admit to you. I told you to throw all those little yellow stones away, but I kept one of them myself. I thought if we ever found your father and Charlie, they might like to look at it."

"Show them one of what?" asked Charlie, who was supporting his bunged-up leg on a hospital cane.

Kayak opened his hand and dropped a heavy yellow nugget on the white bed sheet that covered Mr. Morgan's chest.

"What's that?" asked Charlie.

A strange look came over Mr. Morgan's frost-patched face. "I don't have to touch it. I can smell it. I can even taste it. It's a nugget of pure placer gold. I can feel its precious troy weight like a ton of bricks upon my chest. It's big! It's huge! Wherever that nugget came from there's sure to be a whole lot more."

"*Ahaluna*! Certainly there are many more," said Kayak. "We had to throw them away, didn't we, Mattoosie. We were starving. They were too heavy. We couldn't carry them. We didn't think we'd make it home."

Ross Morgan sat up and stared at his son, Matt. "Do you two mean to say you know where there are more of these?"

"Sure we do," said Matthew.

"Kayak! Matt! Charlie! We're rich! We're super rich, I tell you. You boys may have found the Arctic mother lode."

"It weighs like gold," said Charlie as he bounced the heavy nugget in his hand. Then he kissed it tenderly. "Matt, where did you find this jolly little souvenir?"

"In a river about a hundred miles northwest of here," Matthew answered proudly.

Matthew preferred to be called Matt. He had alert gray eyes and light brown sandy hair. He had shoulders that were growing wider, narrow hips and long straight legs. He had been the fastest runner in his schools in Arizona and in British Columbia. He was not nearly as tall as his father but you could see that he soon would be. He had grown so quickly that almost everything he wore was too small for him.

If his mother had been alive, she probably would have bought new clothing for him. His father thought of different things: of geology, and of wide-ranging schemes for prospecting in the desert or the jungle or the Arctic.

Matthew had moved from place to place with his father. He had attended half a dozen different schools, often in different countries. Now he had found a real friend in Kayak. They had recently become blood brothers, as Kayak, himself, had said. Matthew did not want to lose him.

"Look at him, lads," Charlie said, jerking his thumb toward the dark frost patches on Mr. Morgan's rough, weatherbeaten face. "You are observing a very bad case of gold fever. Matt, your father didn't even touch that little metal treasure before his mind went flying out ahead of his body staking mineral claims. I can see his thoughts are fluttering back and forth trying to find the money and supplies we need and even a good name for his river of gold."

"It's not going to be *my* river of gold," Matt's father said and pointed to Kayak and his son. "It's going to be *their* river of gold. Oh well, maybe if there's lots of it, we could make it *our* gold mine. We could call it Baffin Gold Mine Unlimited, or the Kayak-Morgan Mining Cooperative."

"Or we could call it the Waltzing Matilda Yellow Stone Company," Kayak said.

"Yes." Mr. Morgan laughed. "We could call it anything you like. But let's hurry before someone else gets there and stakes it out in their name. Somebody go and get me the hospital scale. They must have one in the nurses' office down the hall. Don't tell any lies," he called to his son, Matthew. "But . . . but . . . don't tell anyone what it is we want to weigh."

Matthew could see his father start to drift away from him as he dreamed of this new chance to gain a mineral fortune.

When Matt returned and placed the scales upon his father's chest, Mr. Morgan said, "Holy smoke! Do you know, Kayak, that this little yellow stone of yours weighs four and three quarter ounces . . . twelve ounces to the pound troy weight . . . and with gold the price it is . . . phew! Charlie, you could make the down payment for your helicopter repairs with just this single nugget."

"Leaping lizards! I sure could." Charlie sighed. "That is, if it were mine."

"It *is* yours," said Kayak. "Or Mr. Morgan's. I don't want it. Mattoosie found it first and I brought it back to give you. It's only a little sample of the ones we left at the river."

"It's yours, Charlie. Take it," Matt said. "You saved our lives when you flew *Waltzing Matilda* and picked us up off that moving ice. We're only alive and here because of you."

"No, I can't take it," Charlie said. "You two shouldn't go tossing precious gold around."

"Well, you can't refuse a gift," said Kayak. "My people, the Inuit, they think that refusing a gift is about the worst awful thing that anyone can do."

"Remember that, Charlie," Mr. Morgan said.

"Yes. Well . . . maybe I could borrow it . . . but only as a loan so I can patch up old Matilda. She's racked and cracked and she badly needs a few new parts and paint."

Kayak handed Charlie the gold nugget.

"Charlie, you've got to move fast," said Mr. Morgan. "Radio out to Montreal or phone that helicopter company in Connecticut and order everything flown in here to Frobisher. All of you be careful," Matt's father said quietly. "Don't let a single soul know anything about this lucky find of ours."

"Mum's the word," said Charlie, as he slipped the heavy nugget into his breast pocket. "I'm going over right now and give this little yellow egg to Henry. He's the Royal Canadian Mounted Police constable here. He'll keep it in his safe for us and pay Matilda's debtors with it later. Once she's fixed, Matilda can whirl us straight to that river in less than half an hour."

He lifted his bad leg into the air and twirled his cane around his head like a helicopter blade, snatched his harmonica from his hip pocket, played, and sang:

"Waltzing Matilda, Waltzing Matilda,
I'll go awaltzing Matilda with you!"

"Hold it a minute, Charlie," Mr. Morgan said. "We've got to ask these boys exactly where this nugget came from."

"We know," said Kayak.

"Yes, we can show you on a map," said Matt.

"Good," Matthew's father said. "We've got to start to make a plan to get ourselves up there fast so we can stake our claims."

He began to work himself upright so he could get out of bed, but Charlie forced him back just as the nurse came in.

"What's going on in here?" she said. "A football scrimmage? Every one of you except Charlie is supposed to be resting in your beds. And he's supposed to be on crutches. I can't understand you men. One minute you're out prospecting for copper and there's a plane wreck. They bring you in here half-frozen. The next minute Charlie's ducked out and is flying over Frobisher Bay rescuing you boys off the drifting ice in that broken-down whirlybird of his. Now you're all up here huddling around Mr. Morgan like pirates at a picnic. Back to bed," the nurse ordered, "or I'll report you to the doctor."

Kayak and Matthew waved good-by and wandered down the hall. Their legs still felt thin and wobbly. They were glad to climb into their beds.

"I'm hungry," Kayak said.

"Let's ask for another meal. The nurse said that now we could have all the food we want." Matthew sighed. "I wonder if you should have brought that nugget out."

"I wonder, too," said Kayak. "Your dad and Charlie

went kind of crazy when they saw that little piece of gold. Did you see Charlie's eyes? They grew as big as goose eggs. I hope your dad's still going to run a students' tent school this summer to teach geology on Baffin Island."

"I begin to doubt it," said Matt. "When my dad gets thoughts of gold or silver or any precious metal in his head, there's just no stopping him. I've seen him act like this before. I mean when we were prospecting in Arizona and British Columbia and also when we were living in Peru. Remember earlier this spring . . . when he and Charlie thought they'd found that high-grade copper mine? I'm afraid," said Matt, "that nothing will hold them back now. The minute Matilda's flying we'll be away again. You'll see. That gold will draw them like a magnet."

"Mattoosie," Kayak said. "Remember you're my brother now. You can't go away without me. I would kind of worry about you, wandering around, maybe freezing or getting into other troubles in my country. When the doctor lets us out, you better come to my house while I ask my family if they'll let me go away again with you."

Matthew and Kayak were discharged from the Frobisher Hospital on the 27th of May, two days before the doctor would let Charlie and Matt's father out. Matthew went to stay with Kayak's family in their house on Apex Hill above Frobisher Bay.

When they left the little hospital, they noticed that the road to Apex had turned soft, as the new spring warmth spread north across the Arctic Islands.

"*Nelunuktuk*. He says we got to go the bumpy way," said Kayak, interpreting for his cousin, Namoni, who had come to take them home.

Namoni's battered purple snowmobile took them zooming across the rolling snow-packed hills. They stayed clear of the road.

Kayak's house in the Inuit village was small and brightly painted. The snowdrifts around it were melting fast, exposing old skin-drying racks and children's sleds. Appearing through the snow was a well-worn canoe with a rusting outboard motor still screwed onto its stern. On the roof of Kayak's house lay three frozen caribou carcasses safe from the teeth of hungry dogs. Kayak opened the door and Matthew followed him inside.

The house was dark and plain—one big room with two large beds, a small oil stove and a table covered with tin cups and plates and opened biscuit boxes. Kayak's mother sat on one bed sewing. His grandmother sat on the other, her head nodding as she seemed to study the strange forms and patterns created by night frost on the window panes.

"*Shartoalook, kakpoosi?*" Kayak's mother said.

"Mattoosie, my mother she is worried about us. She says we both look awful thin. She thinks we must be hungry. Do you want meat?" asked Kayak.

"I'd like some caribou. Thank you," said Matthew shyly, remembering the importance the Inuit attached to sharing food. "And some tea."

After they had eaten, Kayak's father came in. He smiled at both of them.

Kayak said a lot of things in Inuktitut, often using the word Mattoosie and saying *kungatasho* and *tingmiak* which Matt knew referred to things that fly.

"My father he wants to know," said Kayak, "if I go with you in the up and down bird—that's what he calls a helicopter—how long we going to be away?"

"I don't know," said Matthew. "Maybe most of the summer, if we stake claims on the whole river."

"My mother says she's worried we won't get enough to eat out there. She says I'm only learning to be a hunter. She says I should remember that . . . I'm not a real good hunter yet."

"You tell your mother," Matt said, "that my father's going to buy enough food for everyone and fly it north with us."

Kayak's father spoke to Kayak's grandmother in a soft, gentle voice.

"My dad is telling my grandmother that he once flew in an airplane and thought it was wonderful but quite scary when going up and coming down. My grandmother is laughing at that," said Kayak. "She says she wouldn't mind to try flying. She says she's too old now to be afraid of anything."

The grandmother said a lot to Kayak in a kind old

singsong voice.

Kayak smiled and said, "My *annanachiak,* she's not afraid of airplanes. But she warns us that if we go up north, we should wait for snow and take a sled and a team of dogs with us. In that way, she says, we be pretty sure to get back here sometime, maybe. She says she's seen men go out with sixteen dogs and come staggering back three moons later with only one dog pulling. She says the trouble with airplanes is that they look like birds, but you can't eat them when you're starving. She says dog tastes good, if you are truly hungry."

Kayak added in a whisper to Matthew, "Everything's all right. No one in my family has said yet that I shouldn't go with you." Kayak stood up and smiled. "Let's leave quick, Mattoosie, before they change their minds. We got to go and see our teacher at the school. She told the nurse she wants to talk about how we're going to catch up on all the work we missed. School will be over in less than a month."

Outside, a huge black and white husky dog came shyly toward them, wagging his tail. It was Kayak's dog, Shulu. "I'd like to take him north with us. Do you think Charlie would like that?" Kayak asked.

"I don't think there would be space inside Matilda for the five of us and all the supplies we have to take. That dog is as big as any man."

"Too bad," said Kayak. "What my grandmother says is true. That Shulu might be a good help to us.

He's strong. Come on, Mattoosie. My cousin's gone. We got to walk to school. The teacher said she'd start to help us sharp at four o'clock."

Matt sighed. "Right now I wish we were piling everything into Matilda and going out for gold instead of going to school."

"Me, too," said Kayak. "But don't tell that to her!"

II

SKY ESCAPE

"FINALLY! AT LAST I GOT MY RADIO MESSAGE!" CHARLIE hopped around, waving the telegram above his head. "*Waltzing Matilda*'s parts are coming in on Nordair's flight today. Want to come to the hangar and watch them unload? You two can help me patch up ·the dear old darling. I ordered new red spray paint for her. It's so bright that anyone will be able to see her right from that snowy white mountain over there clear to the west coast of Australia."

"Sure. We'll be glad to help you." Matthew said. "It was good to get out of hospital, but it's even better to be out of school for the summer."

"Fixing Matilda will be fun," Kayak added.

Matthew and Kayak walked beside Charlie to the stripped-down helicopter.

15

"I'll have her flying soon, ready to take us any-where. Speaking of anywhere, has your father ever asked you two to show him on a map exactly where you found . . ."

Charlie made a secret sign to change the subject, as he saw a bulldozer operator come striding toward them across the concrete hangar floor. "Yes"—he laughed, as he unlatched the helicopter's engine cowling—"in the Australian desert up near Alice Springs it's sometimes a wee mite warm and dusty. A pilot out there should be his own engineer. He should be licensed to jolly well maintain his ruddy chopper. That's a sight trickier than just flying these things hither and thither like a lot of doodle bugs."

Charlie drank five thermos bottles of coffee as he worked almost around the clock, helped sometimes by the boys. Three days later, he announced that he had *Waltzing Matilda* "in lovely working order once again."

"I'm all tuckered out," said Charlie, as he showed Kayak and Matt how to put on gauze safety masks.

Taking turns, they carefully spray-painted Matilda a gorgeous shade of cherry red. They stood back to admire her.

"She looks spanking new," said Charlie, "but she's gone and lost her kangaroo-ness. Poor old Matilda could be any one of a hundred different working helicopters. Like a fire engine, she's had a lot of wild experiences." Charlie laughed and patted her new black-plastic-covered seats. "You two have got to do something to make her special."

"I've never even seen a kan-gar-oooo," said Kayak, "but Mattoosie says he's seen kan-gar-oooos in zoos. So between us we could paint one on her side."

"That would be great," said Charlie. "You can start early in the morning. She'll be nice and dry by then."

Working carefully together, Matt and Kayak had outlined and painted their kangaroo by noon. When Matt Morgan's father came into the hangar with Charlie, he stepped back in surprise.

"Skiis—on a kangaroo? Who ever heard of a kangaroo on skiis?"

Charlie said, "And with two joeys in her pouch!"

"Matilda's an Arctic kangaroo," said Kayak proudly.

"You've done it just right," Charlie said. "Matilda loves those skiis. I can feel her quivering to fly again."

"Tonight's the night to get your sleeping bags and packsacks together. Keep your kit small," Ross Morgan said to them. "If the weather's good, we'll load her up with gas and supplies and take off early in the morning when all the gold claim jumpers are lying fast asleep."

Kayak hurried home, ate some delicious seal meat and slept, not knowing when he might return again to his family's house.

Charlie stayed the night with Matt and his father in the unused government house that they had been allowed to occupy rent free. Twice that night Matt got up and went outside to check the weather. The first time his watch said twelve o'clock, the second time a little after two. All night the sky stayed as bright as day.

As he looked at the range of snow blue mountains northwest of Frobisher, he thought, my dad is just like me, lonely without my mother since she died in the car crash in Arizona. But neither of us can change that now. My dad's been out in mountains and deserts searching for gold all his life, and *now*, tomorrow morning, Kayak and I are going to show him the river of frozen fire, with enough gold glistening in it to last us all our lives. While he watched the sun's glow beyond the eastern hills, it seemed to Matthew that the whole world was waiting, listening to the cold, clean wind's song.

The worst fears he had felt about polar bears before he'd seen any had faded from his mind after he had watched a real bear cross the pan of ice on which he and Kayak had been adrift. They had played dead to save their lives. Matthew thought of the terrible adventures he and Kayak had had searching for Charlie and his father after Matilda had crashed, of the wild man they had found, and how lucky they all were to have survived. Then he shivered and hurried back inside the quiet house.

Matt woke again when he heard the door swing open, as Kayak let himself in. Slung over his shoulder Kayak had his red packsack stuffed with clothing and a homemade eiderdown sleeping bag. He wore a new parka that his sister Pia had helped make for him.

She had sewn on handsome wolf-skin trim. He had on new sealskin boots tied tight at the knees with bright green wool ribbons.

"Look, Mattoosie, my grandmother made a new pair of boots for you, too," Kayak whispered. "And my mom sent these." He held up four big, red-bellied Arctic char. "She caught these herself up near the falls. She says eating fish will keep us strong and healthy." Then he added shyly, "I've still got what my girl friend sent me from Kingmerok where she lives," and he held out a small plastic case that contained a mirror.

Ross Morgan and Charlie jumped out of their sleeping bags and started bustling around in their long white winter underwear, stuffing last-minute things into packs and duffle bags. Mr. Morgan began to cook breakfast, but Charlie pulled on his pants, boots and parka and started toward the door.

"Wait and eat something," Matt's father called out to him.

Charlie snatched a pair of fat sausages from the frying pan where they'd just begun to sizzle. "I'll just take a good swig of coffee and gnash on these chubby little bangers on my way down to the hangar. They taste goodo!" He laughed. "Reminds me of breakfast in the Australian Air Force. I'm off to load Matilda. I'll warm her up, then I'll chop on down to the end of the runway and pick up you three chaps. Pip, pip!"

When he left, Ross Morgan chuckled. "I think Charlie's moving fast because he's a wee bit worried about his creditors. They warned him he mustn't fly that helicopter until he'd paid them every penny for all the new parts. Charlie says that unless we fly out and find the gold, they'll never get their second payment."

That thought made the three of them gulp down their breakfast of thick hardtack biscuits, plum jam and banger sausages in a hurry.

"Make sure the stove's turned off," Matt's father said, as he folded up the maps, "and that the thermos bottle's full of coffee. Let's go. Let's go!"

Walking awkwardly because of the loaded packs and sleeping bags they carried on their backs, they hurried down the snow-banked road toward the silent airport. As they approached, they heard Matilda's big blades whirl into life and suddenly they saw her bright red sides flash boldly as she rose above the airport. Just beneath the helicopter they could also see three big men in bulky parkas galloping along the runway, shaking their fists violently upward at Matilda.

"Get moving!" Mr. Morgan shouted. "Run as hard as you can. Charlie wants us to meet him at the end of the runway. He's in one helluva hurry!"

Kayak in his light skin boots easily took the lead as they veered away from the road and took a fast short cut across the gravel banks and tundra.

"Holy smoke!" Ross Morgan shouted. "Those bill collectors are moving quicker than we are. Run faster, Matt. Run faster!"

Charlie was already lowering Matilda. He had the door beside him open. He was gesturing to them wildly. "Get in! Get in!"

Mr. Morgan gasped, "F-f-f-faster! We've got to . . . catch up to . . . Kayak! Those are Charlie's creditors . . . trying to keep him . . . from taking off . . . again."

Kayak was the first to reach Matilda, and flinging his packsack aboard, he nimbly leaped inside. Matt's father, who had been a famous football quarterback, was running well ahead of Matt. Matt saw him duck his broad shoulders beneath the whirling blur of the helicopter's blades, then heave himself aboard Matilda.

"Wait! Wait for me," Matt shouted, and he dashed toward the bright red aircraft.

The three heavy men came gallumping down the airstrip, reaching out to grab Matilda. In desperation Charlie gunned the helicopter's engine. Matilda thundered upward into the ice-blue Arctic sky.

III

THE WILD MAN'S PATH

JUST IN TIME, KAYAK FLUNG A SHORT, STEEL-RUNGED ladder down to Matthew who grabbed it and felt himself drawn upwards until his feet dangled a few inches above the creditors' leaping, clutching, grasping fingers. His father's huge hand reached down and grabbed his bundles, then caught Matt firmly by the point of his parka and hauled him up, safe inside Matilda. Charlie let Matilda dance and hover just beyond the reach of the men below while he waved down at them. He made a "V" for victory sign, then jerked his thumb back toward the Frobisher Mounted Police barracks where the first part of their payment was being held.

"Ruddy overeager beavers, aren't they?" he shouted, as he slid the chopper's door tight shut and gave Matilda a sudden forward thrust. Placing his hand over his heart and grinning widely, Charlie began singing:

"Up jumped the jolly swagmen,
And dashed into the billybong,
We'll go awaltzing Matilda with you."

The three others joined in the chorus:

"Waltzing Matilda,
Waltzing Matilda,
We'll go awaltzing
Matilda with you."

Charlie pressed the stick and Matilda rose triumphantly above the Arctic airstrip. She circled the airport control tower at Frobisher.

"Good luck, Charlie-boy! *Bon chance, mon ami. Bon voyage.* You're going to need it," the man in the control tower called through his microphone.

Charlie made a thumbs-up sign to him.

Matilda zoomed along the shore ice of the bay and circled low around Kayak's house. His whole family came out and waved. His sister Pia ran along below them with his dog Shulu, tail waving, too.

Then they settled down to business. Matt's father unfolded his big map and pointed to the exact spot the boys had marked. The helicopter turned and headed north searching for the steaming falls that would mark the right spot on the river of gold.

"We're up, up and away," Charlie shouted joyfully, clapping Matthew's father on the back. "We're free at last, Ross Morgan. All of us are free to hunt for arctic treasure!"

Matilda thundered north across the coastal range of mountains, still white with snow, that rimmed the inland plain of Baffin Island.

Mr. Morgan examined his map with care. He ran his forefinger along a crooked blue line and shouted to Matt and Kayak who sat behind him. "Is this the way you traveled through the mountains, when you came searching for us?"

"I don't know for sure," said Matthew.

"No," Kayak said, "we came over there, up the Goose River. You can see it going back toward Matilda's tail."

Charlie followed the direction of Kayak's finger, turning north to follow the river through the narrow mountain pass. Before them Matt could see the long lake where he and Kayak had lost the supply of gasoline for their snowmobile. His eyes searched northward.

"There *it* is," said Kayak. "See it?"

Matt showed their abandoned snowmobile to his father and Charlie who changed Matilda's course again, flying low over it.

"It looks dead and lonely," Matthew said.

"I think the weather is rusting it," Kayak answered. "When full summer comes, it will fall through the ice and disappear."

Looking down, they could see that the main body of ice on the lake had open water all around its edges, and some huge cracks and holes were widening in the bright glare of the Arctic sun.

"*Ionamut*," said Kayak. "That means it can't be helped. That Skidoo is lost forever now. No use in worrying. It's like people dying. We can't change the things that happen. That's what my people say. What do the Indians say in Arizoona?"

"I don't know," Matthew said, and silently agreed with Kayak. The Eskimos were right—his mother's death in Arizona was something he couldn't change, no matter how he tried.

"Do you think it was that river down there where you threw back all those golden nuggets?" Ross Morgan pointed at a line of shining water that churned toward a small, partly-frozen lake.

Matt glanced at Kayak who said, "*Ayii*, I think so. But, maybe no. We should see dozens of small waterfalls on the river. Remember, Mattoosie? The air was cold then and only that one big falls was putting up a lot of steam."

"It won't be doing that now," Charlie shouted as he looked at his temperature gauges. "It's warming up out there. You won't see steam today."

Charlie was right. Before them lay the opening tundra with the spring snow fading everywhere. Many different networks of shining lakes and streams, snow ponds and rivers glistened in the midmorning Arctic sunlight. They could not tell the big falls that had steamed during the winter from any of the others.

"Where did you two dump the gold?" Charlie

BIBLIOTHÈQUE PUB. de VANIER

821584

called back to them and removed his head phones, waiting for their answer.

Once again Matt turned and looked at Kayak who sat alert, his eyes flickering back and forth across the tundra and the many twisting water courses that lay before them.

"I . . . I don't know," said Kayak. "It's not at all the same up here in summer as it was with the two of us walking down there in winter with snow drifted all around, hiding all but the strongest rivers."

"I'll land Matilda, when you think we're getting close," said Charlie. "And you, Ross Morgan," he said to Matthew's father, "you start sniffing with that famous broken footballer's nose of yours. You always told me you could smell gold if I flew you past it."

"I don't trust my nose today." Matthew's father laughed. "And anyhow, we're too high up. I think you'd better land. We don't want to overfly this golden river."

"Look!" yelled Matthew, pointing. "I think I saw yellow metal glinting in the bottom of that river. Could that be the place where we threw all the nuggets?"

"Hold on to your hats," shouted Charlie, and he adjusted the controls.

Matilda lost altitude, then hovered like a fish hawk just above the river. They landed on the bank. Kayak opened the door.

"This has got to be the place," said Matthew as he jumped out.

Ducking carefully beneath Matilda's whirling blades, the boys ran along the river bank.

"Everything looks so different now without the snow," Kayak said to Mr. Morgan, when he joined them. "But perhaps Mattoosie's right. This may be the very spot. It's hard to tell a place in summer when you have only seen it covered up with snow."

Matthew knelt and reached down into the ice-cold, rushing river. The stone he lifted out was pure yellowish quartz without a trace of any metal. He took out another and another, but threw them back again.

"We must be wrong," said Matthew to his father. "There were gold nuggets lying everywhere in the riverbed we saw."

"It's true," said Kayak. "You could see them glittering all along the river bottom just like the one we brought to you. Mattoosie, this must be a different river. Maybe the one we're looking for is over there."

Kayak and Matthew ran across the tundra and carefully searched the waters to the east and west. Charlie and Mr. Morgan, meanwhile, flew very low and slow along a dozen nearby river courses. They saw not one speck of gold.

When they returned, Matthew said, "Oh, Dad!" and his voice was full of disappointment. "We've gone and lost that river. We only found it in the first place because the wild man pointed out the way for us to find the steaming falls."

"We could wait until next winter," Charlie said.

"If it's near a waterfall," said Mr. Morgan, "the action of the rushing water could sweep away that gold or cover it with silt and gravel. We should try to find it soon."

"Then come on, quick," Charlie said. "Don't get discouraged. Everybody into old Matilda and we'll go up and have another look."

Again they saw absolutely nothing.

That evening they made camp, setting up two red nylon sleeping tents on a dry gravel bank. They wolfed down their rations and drew a careful grid on Mr. Morgan's map. Then, for three whole days they searched by foot along the river courses. Nothing helped. Matt's father analyzed his map. "We must be searching the wrong river beds," he said. "None of these show any signs of precious metal."

"I wish we would see that owl again, or find the wild man's house," said Matthew. "He would tell us where to find the gold."

"Don't worry!" Charlie laughed. "It's the luck of the prospecting game. Fortunes in placer gold are hard to find these days. But you hear this, old chummy," he said to Matthew's father, "the gasoline we flew in here is nearly finished and poor Matilda will soon be dying of the thirst. I know of a good-sized government gas cache not too far northeast of here. I jolly well better go and rustle up some aviation petrol or we'll find ourselves helping each other to stagger home on foot." He ran his hand along his still-stiff leg. "That's a thought I don't exactly fancy."

"You can't load those av-gas drums yourself," Ross Morgan said. "They weigh four hundred and fifty pounds apiece. I'll come along and help you." He glanced at his wristwatch. It was just after seven o'clock. "Do you boys mind staying here in camp tonight and waiting for us?"

Matt looked at Charlie and his father. "No, we don't," he said, "but this time don't get lost."

"Don't worry," said Charlie. "The weather's clear and we can fly every hour of the clock up here this time of year. We'll be back safe and sound before you're up and have had your breakfast. Put on the tea kettle, when you hear Matilda come chopping through the ozone this time tomorrow morning."

Charlie gunned his dear old waltzer's engine. Matilda rose into the thin clear air and her whirling blades made a wind that billowed the red tents like sails and nearly blew them flat.

"It's really silent out here with them gone," Matthew said. "Do you feel like sleeping?"

"No," answered Kayak. "I'd like to go and walk along some of those caribou trails I showed you from Matilda's window."

"I'm ready," said Matt. "Let's go."

Kayak and Matthew tied the tent flaps loosely shut and walked northwest. They climbed a small hill where Matt stopped and looked across the enormous island landscape cut by low hills and sudden cliffs.

To the north the island disappeared in the shimmering haze of the far horizon. To the west he could see the long curving shoreline still gripped by miles of smooth white sea ice. Beyond that lay the glittering blue waters of Foxe Basin, choked with long chains of drifting pack ice moving slowly southward into Hudson Bay. Most of the snow had melted off the land, leaving all the south slopes bare, exposing the endless plains of striped rock in fading shades of gray and brown and granite red. Woven in among the rocks were mounds of gravel—eskers—and wide patches of tundra with caribou moss just beginning to lose its winter drabness and take on brighter summer hues. Everywhere there were ponds reflecting the open sky.

Kayak said, "Enjoy our land, Mattoosie. Look anywhere, look everywhere and you will see why Inuit love this whole great country where we live."

They could hear the wild, high crying of a pair of falcon that swept on sharp white wings across the land.

"This is one of the best times of all the year out here on the tundra," Kayak said. "It's not cold and yet the mosquitoes have only come a little and it stays light so you can see all night. Listen! You hear the geese?"

Kayak pointed high into the air at a long wedge of the big birds flashing their snowy wings against the deep blue of the evening sky.

"*Kungo! Kungo!*" he called up to them, and they

answered him, *"Kungo, kungo, kungo."*

"Mattoosie, you should speak to them, too," Kayak said. "It's good luck to speak back to the first snow geese that see you. Makes them know you're glad to see them coming home to nest."

They had not gone very far before Kayak stopped and said, "Mattoosie, can you see the trails now?"

Matt looked all around him and said, "No."

"Look at that small hill. See the straight lines through the tundra?"

They hurried to the place.

"There must have been lots of caribou to make such a rutted path," Matt said.

They followed along the deepest caribou trail for some distance when suddenly Kayak stopped and said, "I think we've found him."

"Found who?" Matthew asked.

"The wild man," Kayak whispered, crouching down. "Look over there!"

IV

I C E C A V E

"I DON'T SEE ANYTHING SPECIAL EXCEPT THAT PILE OF stones," said Matthew.

"Do you know any animals that pile up stones?" asked Kayak.

"No," said Matthew.

"I think you'll see," Kayak said, "that some human arranged those stones like that."

When they reached the man-sized rough pyramid of rocks, Kayak climbed up and looked inside.

"Nothing in there now," he said.

"What is it?" Matthew asked.

"It's a fox trap, the kind Inuit used a long time ago. They'd throw in a piece of meat for bait and later a white fox would hop down inside and not be able to jump out again. When that fox started yipping and yapping, other foxes would come and jump in with him. Sometimes hunters would find a single trap full of foxes."

Matt looked at the empty trap and said, "Do you mean maybe somebody built this three hundred years ago?"

"Yes, I think so," Kayak said. "The moss and the weather on most of the stones show that. But what about these?" He pointed to a dozen stones near the top of the trap.

"They are a different color," Matt admitted. "No lichen on them."

"Yes," said Kayak. "They're different because some human repaired that trap only a couple of years ago, maybe even yesterday. It's hard to tell. Mattoosie, do you believe the wild man fixed that fox trap?"

"I don't know," said Matthew. "Would that mean his hidden house is near us now?"

"No," said Kayak. "But maybe this trap will help us find it. If we could talk to him, he could surely tell us where to find the gold."

"How can that stone trap help us find his house?"

"I'll show you. But first we've got to look for the next fox trap. Let's hurry," Kayak said. "We got to climb that hill before the valleys grow too dark. Even though it's light all night, the shadows in the valleys will make it hard to see."

They crossed the long rolling tundra plain as it turned golden in the setting sun. Matthew was puffing for breath by the time they reached the hill crest. Kayak, who was wearing his new knee-high sealskin boots, was able to move faster. Matthew wished again that he had worn his instead of heavy steel-toed boots.

"I think I see it." Kayak pointed to a dark spot that must have been almost a mile away.

They hurried on.

"It *is* another fox trap," Kayak said, as Matt caught up.

"I see that," answered Matt, "and someone has repaired this one as well."

"Now you're using your eyes," said Kayak. "You're learning lessons my father taught me, lessons we would never learn in school."

"I still don't see how these two traps will help us find the wild man's house."

"If a hunter wants to move over a long distance, walking or with a dog team, he usually travels in a straight line. Even the foxes do that. When you see their tracks on snow, unless they're hungry, they'll usually be going sort of straight. Now, Mattoosie, point between this trap and the one we found before."

Matt turned and pointed south.

"Good," said Kayak. "Now, where's the next trap going to be, if there is one?"

Matt lined up the two traps. He then pointed straight north, far beyond them.

"Yes," said Kayak. "It should be so. I think we'll

see the next one almost exactly where you're pointing."

"This is like a treasure hunt," said Matthew. He
looked at his wristwatch. "It's nearly ten o'clock at
night. Maybe we should go back to the tent and wait
for Dad and Charlie."

"It's a long way back there," said Kayak. "They're
not due until tomorrow morning, and if they return
early, we would hear Matilda. I'd like to see if that
third trap is where we think it is and if it has been
repaired, too."

"You're like a detective," Matt said. "You like to
search and find each clue."

"That's the way a hunter has to be, if he wants to
stay alive." Kayak waved his hands across the rocky
landscape. "Mattoosie, there's nobody out here to tell
us anything. We got to discover everything we wish
to know all by ourselves."

It was after eleven o'clock by the time they came
to the third empty fox trap, exactly where Kayak and
Matthew had guessed it would be. Bright rocks
showed where it, too, had been repaired. Kayak and
Matt sat down, resting their backs against the high
stone trap.

"My legs feel like they're falling off," said Matt.
"I wish I'd worn those light sealskin boots your
grandmother made for me."

"Do you see the trail going over that hill?" asked
Kayak.

"Another caribou trail." Matt sighed. "There's lots of them."

"I don't think that's a caribou trail," said Kayak. "Caribou got sharp hooves that cut a path. That trail's soft. It's made in kind of an 'S' shape, like a man makes not wanting to slide on the tundra in his skin boots. See the way it shines in the long light. That trail was made not long ago." Kayak got quickly to his feet. "It was made after the snow had left the ground. Come on. Let's follow it."

As soon as they reached level ground on the other side of the hill, Kayak and Matthew knew where they were.

"It's the wild man's underground house all right." Kayak stuck his head down the entrance hole. "But it's deserted." His voice was filled with disappointment. "He's gone. He told us he would go, because he feared the airplane men would come and find him once we knew his hiding place."

"He was right," said Matthew sadly. "We did come back to hunt him out just as he said we would."

Matt looked at the ruin of the old house. It was like looking at a rough, round basement, dug into the ground, with the ribs of a big whale arched over it like the roof rafters in a house.

"He had those whale ribs covered with thick seal-skins and tundra and snow so that his house was hidden underground in winter. Remember? That's how the old Baffin Island Tunik people used to build their main houses. The wild man loves the old ways best."

"He didn't take too much with him," Matthew said. "He left those old rusty red reflectors and the U.S. Army jeep license plates and Canadian Air Force ration boxes and chewed-up bones and caribou antlers and wild goose feathers. He must have left here in a hurry."

"And not so long ago," said Kayak.

He bent down and looked at the faint footprints the wild man and his family had left, crushed down in the tundra. Matthew, too, could see that they were heading north.

"It's a long way back to the tent to sleep," said Kayak. "Let's curl up near here, where it's dry, and rest."

Even though the brighter light of dawn was already creeping through the eastern sky, Matthew shivered as he felt the cold night wind whip around them. He was tired.

"We haven't any covers, but you can curl around that stone," said Kayak. "Be careful not to touch it. Stones are cold unless they're in the sun. Just curl around it to protect your body from the wind. Then if the wind shifts, you shift, too, so the wind's full strength won't hit you. It's a woman's trick my mother taught me. It's a good way to sleep out on the land when you got no sleeping skins with you. Put your parka on backwards, Mattoosie, the way

I'm doing it, and pull your arms inside, out of your sleeves, and hug your body," Kayak said. "Now pull your hood up over your face and let your breath go down around your body. It will help to keep you warm. If you get too cold, your feet will wake you up. Then you got to jump up and run and flap your arms like a duck till you feel warm again."

Matthew bedded down around a stone as he was told and within a few minutes both boys were sleeping soundly, so soundly they did not hear the thunking of Matilda's noisy, whirling blades as the helicopter flew in toward their distant camp.

When Matthew awoke, he felt a chill on his left side seeping up from the cold ground and yet his right side was heated by the by-now strong yellow sunlight of the Arctic morning. He saw Kayak quickly reverse his parka. He pulled a small package of raisins and two large hardtack biscuits from their pack. They shared these and drank cold clear water from a pond.

"If my mom were here," said Matthew, "she'd say, 'Sonny, brush your teeth.' "

"Mattoosie, you could go back to our tents, if you want to," Kayak said. "You just follow the fox traps. They will lead you to camp. I'm going right now and try to find the wild man. We brought your father and Charlie out here by promising we would show them gold. But we can't find it. The wild man's the only one who knows exactly where it is."

Matthew looked back over the rolling tundra

country with snow still clinging to the north sides of the hills. He was not at all sure he *could* find his way to their small red tents.

"No, I'll come with you," he said. "But we've got to hurry. We should have left a note for Dad and Charlie so they wouldn't worry."

Kayak was already on his feet and moving fast to warm himself, heading into the north, following the wild man's trail.

It was nearly noon, when they came to a huge crack in the granite ridge they were following. The crack was filled with solid ice.

"I've heard about that kind of frozen place," Kayak said as he pointed to the ice fault between the two steep walls of granite, "but I never thought I'd see one. My father told me that the ice hardly melts at all in one of these," said Kayak. "It's so strong and thick and old and shaded by the stone cliffs on either side that it just stays like that, only dripping a little bit in summer. Then winter comes and builds it up and makes it hard as flint again."

"It looks like a small glacier," said Matt. "My father would call it a fissure."

Kayak studied the ice fault carefully. "It's no good to try and cross it here. We'll have to go to that narrow place." He pointed at a faint crushed trail in the tundra.

Matt nodded in agreement.

"I think that's what the wild man did," said Kayak. They walked along the edge of the cliff until they came to a narrow path with well-worn stepping places that led down the glacial ice fault. Cautiously, they moved forward, ducked under an ice ledge and found themselves inside a hollow cave. It was not very cold, but everything was wrapped in blue-green shadows. Sharp icicles hung from the roof of the cave. Water dripped steadily from them like the tick-tick-ticking of some ancient clock.

"This place makes me a little nervous," Matthew whispered.

"Me, too," said Kayak. "I never saw an ice cave like this before in all my life. This is the kind of hidden den where Igtuk the boomer lives. That's what my grandmother told us when we were listening to the winter stories."

"Who's Igtuk the boomer?" Matthew asked him.

"He's a mountain spirit who causes ice slides. He goes '*Igk-Igk-Igk*,' until the awful sound is so loud it breaks your ears right off your head."

"You don't believe that, do you?" Matthew whispered.

"When I'm sitting in school at Frobisher," Kayak whispered back, "I don't believe it and I laugh about those old grandfather stories with most of the other kids. But now that I'm down inside this ice cave, well . . . I believe in Igtuk. How about you?"

"It's hard not to," Matthew said, and shivered. "Down here I believe in everything." His words echoed, *Thing—thing—thing*.

"Talk softly." Kayak shuddered. "I hate the way

our voices echo." *Echo-echo!* "It makes these ice walls seem to answer." *Answer-answer!*

Together, step by step, they crept deeper and deeper into the frightening, crouching shadows of the cave. The cold ice passage seemed to go on forever.

"It's got to end somewhere," Kayak said at last. *Where—where—where!*

"I wish we'd brought the flashlight," Matthew whispered.

At that very moment, something spun down and hit him a stunning blow on the head. Even as he fell, he saw Kayak go crashing down also. The awful sound of high-pitched, crazy laughter echoed through the blue ice cave.

V

SNOW SPIDERS

MATT LAY ON THE ICE FLOOR OF THE CAVE. EVEN THE
thickness of his parka hood had not prevented the
bump that he felt rising on his head. Suddenly he
saw a strange movement high above him. A curious,
creepy-looking ball of fur was descending. Could it
be a huge spider lowering itself on a long thin white
strand? When it reached the ice floor, the hairy
creature scuttled over and examined Kayak who lay
unconscious from the blow that had knocked him
down.

The small furred figure paused only for a moment,
then whirled around and rushed at Matthew. Before
he could move to defend himself, a long white noose
was slipped round his feet and ankles and he felt
himself jerked into the air. Hanging upside down,

he was hauled upwards, swaying back and forth like the pendulum of a clock. He held his hands in front of his face to protect himself from the icicles that hung like long silver daggers from the ceiling's dome.

Matthew was hauled up roughly through a dark hole and dumped onto the frozen floor of a high chamber whose walls were formed from glacial ice and frosted stone. He took his hands away from his eyes and peered into the shadows. There before him stood the wild man, straining with all his might, as he hauled first Kayak and then the furry white creature up into the high ice chamber.

The wild man laughed when he got hold of Kayak by the ankles, untied the noose and sent him slithering across the icy floor. In a minute Kayak came to rest near Matthew.

"So, it's the pair of you, is it? Following me around again." *Again—again!* He was shouting. "Even though I warned you not to do it." *Do it—do it!* His voice went echoing through the cave.

Matthew thought of his last meeting with the wild man and his family. How could he ever forget that big touseled head of hair set on a short, powerful body, covered in old-fashioned caribou pants and parka. The wild man peered into Matthew's face and then shook his head in a way that sent his shaggy mane of black hair flying around his wide brown cheekbones and rattled the hanging band of fox teeth he had strung across his forehead.

The wild man scowled and his dark eyes narrowed.

"I warned you two not to follow me," he said, and clamped his heavy jaw tight shut. Then he laughed in his crazy way, snapping his words out through his square white teeth. "When you go back, you tell the Air Force people that they made it wrong." *Wrong— wrong!* "I hate the way this white parachute cord of theirs stretches. It's light to carry and it's strong enough, but the sealskin lines we make are better. Ashevak, you coil that nylon line," he shouted to the little furry creature whom Matt now recognized as the wild man's son dressed from head to foot in parka, pants and boots of pure white fox skins.

"I ask you, little Kayak and what's your name— Mattoosie"—the wild man laughed and shook the fringe of fox teeth around his head—"how did you two ever find this hidden cave? I thought I was safe from everyone in a distant place like this." He roared again in a way that sent a hundred echoes bounding off the icy chamber walls. "It's like the Inuit say in Frobisher—there's just no escaping from the white men once they start trailing after you." *You—you!*

"We're not hunting after you," said Matthew in a humble voice. "We were just in this part of the country looking around for . . . well, for . . ."

"Yes? Why don't you say it, cousin. Say it! You're out searching for that Baffin Island gold. You probably got radios and airplanes and other white men with you. Is that not true?" *True—true.*

"It is true, sir. But . . ."

"But nothing!" the wild man shouted. "I had to

move once before because of you two." *Hoo—hoo two—two—two!* He pointed his rough, scarred finger at Kayak who had just regained his senses and was sitting up with one hand held against his ear. "And now I guess I got to move again. But *where?*" *Where —where?*

Matthew saw the wild man's wife peeking out from the shadows. She held her youngest child by the hand. She too was dressed from head to toe in furry white fox skins.

"You go back to your lamp, woman, and don't you offer this pair of troublemakers any food this time. They ain't welcome! You hear *me?*" *Me—me?*

"*Ahaluna,* I hear you, because you shout so loud," his wife answered in a voice that was soft and kind. "I am certainly going to feed something to those two boys. Look at them. They've come a long way and they must be hungry. Come on, dear boys, follow me." She smiled. "I have a lovely goose-foot jelly soup heating over my lamp and some fresh raw caribou. I'll gladly give you tender slices."

"Don't let those two slurp it all up and leave me not a drop," the wild man grumbled. "I want some of that goose-foot soup, too, you know." *Know— know.*

When they had shared the food together, Matthew could see that the wild man was in a much better mood. But he was still mumbling and shaking his head, causing the fox teeth that hung across his fore-head to rattle like dry bones.

Finally Kayak got up his nerve and said, "when we left your old house last time and we were walking south, we found those yellow stones in the river and Mattoosie carried them as far as he could. But they were so heavy he had to throw them away. And now" —Kayak laughed nervously—"now we want them and we can't find them. We can't even find the river that you showed us because the devil's winter kettle isn't steaming any more."

"So," the wild man bellowed. "That's why you came back to hunt me down. Well, I ain't telling you a second time! Forget about the gold," he growled. "Be on your way. And don't tell those people living in Frobisher that you've even seen me, understand?"

Kayak took a last gulp of the delicious soup and said to Matthew, "I guess he means it's time for us to go."

"Time?" the wild man shouted. "Time? I hate to hear that awful word." He pushed up his parka sleeves to show the dozen gold and silver wristwatches that he wore on both his arms. "Who cares about white man's time?"

"Husband, you don't fool me." His wife giggled. "You love the look of all those fancy timepieces strapped onto your wrists and arms even though I saw you plucking off the hands of those little clocks and throwing them outside in the snow." She laughed and said to Kayak, "He doesn't like those little tick-tock toys telling him when to wake and eat and sleep.

He says it's their tiny ticking that makes him so wild!" *Wild—wild!*

"Do you think he'll mind if we just slip away? I mean, slip down the spider rope?" Matt whispered. "You tell him we've got to go and find my father."

"Lower the parachute lines," the wild man's wife called out to their white fox-coated children.

"Tug-va-oo-si alun-asee," called Kayak.

"Goodby, everyone," Matthew echoed in Inuktitut, as he clutched the long white lines and went sliding past the icicles to the lower floor of the cave.

"This place I don't like too much," said Kayak. "Let's get out of here before ice chunks start falling on our heads again."

As they hurried away, Matt looked back and saw the wild man's children giggling and hauling up the long white lines. It was good to breathe the air of the open tundra once again.

"Why did the wild man call me cousin?" Matt asked Kayak.

"Because you are his cousin," Kayak replied.

"I didn't know that," Matthew said.

"Don't you know about our great-great grand-mother who built a sealskin slipper that was as big as a boat? In it she put half of her family, the children who were pale, had bushy eyebrows and big ears. Oh, yes," said Kayak, "every Inuit knows she sent them sailing to the south, saying, 'You shall be good at making weapons!' That's how the *kalunait,* the white people, got started in this world, and now you come back to us. And what that old lady said about you making weapons, it was true. That rifle your father left in the tent is really good. We never made anything more wonderful than that."

"Wonderful, yes." Matthew laughed. "That's a fantastic story. But it's not the way we heard that our ancestors appeared. What happened to the other half of that old old woman's children?"

"Oh, they stayed right here in the north. They became *Inuit, the people,* who grew up to be igloo-builders, hunters, carvers, singers, dancers, listeners at the breathing places in the ice, all my closest relatives and family."

Matt thought about the grandmother's story as they walked across the miles of rolling tundra toward the place where they had pitched their tent. Finally they crossed the last hill.

"She's back. Matilda's back!" Kayak shouted when they reached the high ground.

"I'm glad to see her sitting there beside our tents," Matthew said. "It's good to be home again. We must have walked thirty miles in these last two days. My legs feel like a pair of worn-out rubber bands."

The zipper on the tent went sliding up and Charlie and Matt's father stepped outside.

"Here they come," said Charlie; that pair of wandering wallabies who don't know how to write a note to tell their chums when they'll be back. Your father has been very worried," he said to Matt.

"How did you get that bump on the side of your head?" Matt's father asked.

"We went and found him," Matthew answered. "We found the wild man."

"*Ayii,*" said Kayak. "His wife gave us some caribou, and goose-foot soup. But he wouldn't tell us where the golden river was, and he warned us to be off and not come back again."

"Still," said Matt's father, "he seems to be our surest chance of finding all those golden nuggets."

"He lives only about four hours walk from here, in an ice cave," Matthew said, as he slumped down exhausted on the tundra in front of the tents.

"That's only a few minutes ride in little old Matilda." Charlie chuckled. "One of you sit up front with me and point the way," Charlie called to Kayak and to Matthew.

They climbed inside the helicopter and Charlie gunned her engine. Matilda roared into life. Her big blades rotated slowly at first, then disappeared into a whirling silver blur caught by the sun.

It was easy enough finding the huge ice fault that ran through the valley and the place to enter, which was exactly where it narrowed.

"Don't land too close," Kayak warned Charlie. "I don't know what he'll do, if he sees all four of us. He hates flying machines and white man's time and towns with people crowded close together. That's why they live out here, alone."

When Matilda touched the tundra and her engine

was shut down, Mr. Morgan was the first one out.

"Look at that." Charlie laughed. "Real prospectors move mighty fast when they've got gold fever."

As they stepped through the entrance to the blue ice cave, Matt whispered to his father, "Don't laugh or say anything when you see the little white furry creatures who are working the two spider lines."

Matthew's father looked at him in utter disbelief. "Matt, does that bump on the side of your head hurt you? What do you mean white spiders working webs?"

"He's telling you the truth," said Kayak, "about those furry creatures."

"I think you two have both gone bonkers," Charlie said. "Perhaps a crazy shadow cave like this could drive a man to . . . laughing like a loon." *Loon— loon.* ". . . Or even flying upside down." *Down— down.*

"Helloooo up there!" Kayak's voice echoed through the frozen chambers. He pointed at a heavy sealskin line that hung down from the icy upper room. "Perhaps they're all asleep."

"He won't answer us," said Matthew, and he went and jerked gently on the heavy rawhide line. Then he pulled on it with all his strength. The long sealskin cord held fast.

"I'll go up first," said Kayak. "I hope he's not just waiting to bang me on the head again."

Matt's father boosted Kayak up high.

"You be careful," he said as Kayak grasped the

rawhide line and climbed it sailor-style until he disappeared through the blue-green hole among the hanging icicles.

"Dad," whispered Matthew. "He called me cousin. Does that mean you're the wild man's uncle?"

"I think this whole thing is a crazy dream," his father said.

They all three looked upward nervously until they saw Kayak's head reappear above them. There was a look of fear upon his face.

VI

YELLOW KNIFE

"THE WILD MAN AND HIS FAMILY—THEY ARE GONE," Kayak called down to them. "Everything they owned has disappeared. He left only one thing behind, and maybe that's a warning." *Warning—warning.*

"You'd better come down out of there," called Matthew.

"Our luck is running dead against us," Matthew's father shouted.

He and Charlie steadied the rope as Kayak slithered down.

"Are you two sure," asked Charlie, "that you didn't go to sleep and have a dream?" *Dream—dream.*

Matthew's father nodded. "I guess we've been hoodwinked about the gold. We're never going to find it. Gold always seems to get away from me."

Kayak looked at his friend, Mattoosie, then reached down into the top of his high skin boot and said, "I told you the wild man left only one thing up there in his ice cave. It's blade was pointing west."

He drew out a long knife with a curious double-curved hilt. He handed it to Mr. Morgan who held it up. It winked and twinkled yellow in the shifting shadows.

"Holy smoke!" exclaimed Mr. Morgan. "This whole heavy knife has been hammered out of *solid gold!* I saw one of these knives once a long time ago. I never dreamed I'd hold one in my hands." He gave it back to Kayak. "You sure there's nothing else left up there?"

"Nothing," said Kayak. "I searched everywhere. It's empty. He's taken every other thing. He's gone."

"Let's go," Matt's father whispered. But even though his voice was low, the whole ice cave seemed to whisper, echoing back his words. *Let's go—let's go—let's go!*

"This place gives me the willies," Charlie said. It's like some cavern hidden underneath the sea. I didn't think humans could live inside a frozen place like this."

They turned and hurried toward the light.

As soon as they stepped outside the cave, Mr. Morgan said to Kayak, "Try to find their footprints. Look for any sign that will tell us which way they went from here."

Kayak searched with care, but the wild man had

been careful and left not a single clue to show them the direction he was heading.

"Maybe we'll see his path pressed down in the tundra," Kayak said.

"Or maybe, if we circle wide, we could spot him from the air," suggested Charlie. "He can't be all that far from here."

"Hurry, let's go," Mr. Morgan shouted, and they ran to the place where rosy red Matilda sat waiting for them, shining in the morning sun.

Matilda whirled her blades and rose and turned, swooped and hovered over the entrance to the ice cave. They could see nothing but their own crushed paths across the tundra. Charlie guided Matilda in a series of widening circles, moving clockwise into the north, east, south, west. But they saw no other human sign.

"I don't see how he did it," Kayak said. "He's slipped away from us again. When I was in Frobisher, I asked my father about him. He said the wild man used to be the cleverest of hunters. My grandmother said that he thinks fast. I guess that's why he slips away from us."

"This yellow knife," said Kayak, "must have been left by the wild man as a special sign for us. It pointed west."

"It's like a riddle," Matthew said. "Do you suppose the wild man wants us to go west?"

"Or," Charlie warned them, "maybe this knife warns us not to go west at all."

"If you were the wild man," Matt's father asked Kayak, "how would you go?"

"I've never been west of here," Kayak answered. "I would have to follow the *inukshuks*. That's our word for *stone men*. They are markers our people built to help with hunting and to guide our traveling. My grandfather told me that some *inukshuks* point the way to a secret place. He said I would see many standing stone men and that they would tell me something."

"Where is that place where stone men talk?" said Charlie.

"It's west of here," Kayak answered. It's called *Inuk-shuk-sha-lik.*"

"Phew!" gasped Charlie. "I can't even pronounce a name like that. Is it marked on any map?"

"No, I don't think it's on any map," said Kayak. "It's a very ancient Inuit place. It's a very secret place."

"Would it be wrong for you to guide us to it?" Matthew's father asked.

"Who knows," said Kayak. "I don't remember my grandfather saying it would be wrong to take others there. He wanted me to go and listen to what the stone men have to say."

"Let's go," said Charlie. "Let's solve the riddle. If your stone men are pointing west, that's the right direction for Matilda. There's a Mounted Police gas cache about halfway across Baffin Island and they gave me permission to use as much as I need to keep this old girl flying. I promised that I'd repay them later."

They flew back to camp and packed all their gear into the helicopter. "Everybody in," said Charlie, as he roared Matilda's blades.

They rose and whirled away into the west.

"There's one! Down there!" cried Kayak, peering out of Matilda's bubble window. "It's the first stone man."

Charlie lowered Matilda until she hovered near the *inukshuk*. Its stubby arm was pointing west along a narrow path through the tundra.

"Don't bother landing," Kayak said. "Follow that path and let's see where it leads us."

They flew west for almost twenty miles before they found the second stone man. It, too, was facing west.

"You can see where the path leads." Charlie pointed. "Over to that snow-filled valley on the north side of the mountains."

"Keep on going," said Ross Morgan. "Imagine us finding these ancient sign posts in this wild country."

When they saw the third stone man, Matt's father tapped Charlie's shoulder and called out, "What a beautiful country! Look down there. It's a prospector's dream come true. All geologists would love it. There are no trees or bushes, almost no cover on the rocks. Even plain earth, which we call overburden, gets in the true rock hunter's way. But here the early glaciers have stripped everything away. You can see the red iron in those rocks beneath us, and look, lots of black hematite over there, and there's another stone man pointing west. Holy smoke! Just look at those long veins of galena gleaming in the rocks. That's lead," Ross Morgan said. "And in those short cliff faces you can see a lot of sheet mica shining in the morning sun. And those orange traces dipping into that blue-green lake may be indicating copper. I don't like to mention copper —we nearly got killed when we went hunting that!"

As Charlie flew Matilda across Amadjuak Bay, he shouted, "You can see the old Hudson's Bay trading post down there." He pointed at a flagpole and the weathered roof on an abandoned house. "The police gas cache is not far north of here."

Fifteen minutes later they could see the dull red patch made by the hundred drums of aviation gas standing on Lake Mingo's southern shore.

"I'll fill Matilda's gas tanks full," said Charlie. "Then if we squeeze up, we may have room to carry two full drums of gas. We're certainly going to need it, and more later."

"Later?" Kayak laughed. "My grandfather told me to live the best life I could live every single day because nobody really knows if they'll be alive tomorrow."

They took off after refueling and flew again until they could see the western coastline of Baffin Island.

Charlie zoomed Matilda low over another lichen-covered stone figure. "There's another stone man pointing toward that jut of land."

Kayak nodded and looked north and south along the coast. Heavy sea ice stretched away as far as they could see. In the distant haze of the Foxe Basin, shadowy blue Arctic waters were broken by long skeins of ice drifting slowly southward beneath a lead-gray line of heavy fog.

"It should be near here, if I remember what my grandfather told me," Kayak said.

Charlie lowered Matilda and she went skimming along only a stone's throw above the summer tundra.

"What's that over there?" Matthew shouted. "It looks like a graveyard full of tombstones.

Kayak turned and looked. "That's it! That's it! That's what we're looking for. Be careful, Charlie. Don't you land too close."

"OK, here we go," said Charlie. "I'll be glad to get down ahead of that heavy fog that's rolling in."

He lowered Matilda onto a low dry knoll not a hundred paces from the ice-strewn shore.

"Let's go and have a look," said Matthew's father.

Charlie shut down Matilda's engine and they all hurried over to the strangely silent place. Heavy fog was swirling in like smoke among the countless upright stone markers. Each marker was made from many stones wedged together looking like a head, torso, arms and legs.

"They look," said Matthew, "just like groups of frozen people standing, waiting."

"Do you notice that nearly all of them are pointing to the west?" Ross Mogan asked.

"That's what my grandfather told me they'd be doing." Kayak said. "Most of them are pointing at some place across the sea."

"I never thought I'd see a sight like this," Charlie said in wonder. "Those ghostly looking stone men give me the willies."

"We're not alone," Kayak whispered, and he crouched down.

The others did the same.

"Look over there among those farthest statues. Do you see something moving?"

They watched and wondered as they saw something white and furry moving in the cold gray fog, sneaking between one stone man and another. It crept toward them.

"A white fox," said Kayak. "He's just starting to shed his thick winter coat. He's coming over to us because he's not afraid. He's never seen a human being before."

The white fox came and sat so close Matt could almost have reached out and touched it. It sniffed their unfamiliar smell, then turned and delicately trotted off again in search of lemmings.

"This fog is way too thick for flying," Charlie said. "I hope it blows away tomorrow."

They stiffened as they heard the lonely howling of an Arctic wolf beyond the gray stone figures. It was answered by another that was much too close to them. The sound echoed eerily in the drifting fog.

Kayak peered into the heavy mists. "The wolves could be telling each other how many of us have arrived and guessing how our flesh will taste."

The nearest wolf let out another fearsome howl. Kayak lit the pressure lamp in a hurry. He held it high above his head. The hissing lantern's light turned the night fog into a ghostly swirling wall of white that pressed in all around them. Through the fog the yellow eyes of half a dozen wolves watched the strangers hungrily.

VII

A HAIRY STRANGER

"I'M READY TO QUIT THIS RUDDY HEAP OF FROZEN rocks and we haven't yet set up our tents," said Charlie. "I don't half like the looks these friendly neighbors gave us, and I don't appreciate their howlings of complaint. If it weren't for this blooming night fog, I'd take off this very minute."

"Wait!" said Kayak. "My father told me that healthy wolves are not usually dangerous to people. It is just their howling that is frightening."

Mr. Morgan nodded. "I don't like wolves breathing down my neck either. Bring the rifle and we'll all go back to Matilda and get everything we need."

They worked quickly setting up the tents. Kayak crawled inside after Matt and zipped the nylon en-

61

trance tight behind them.

Matthew listened to the sound of heavy paws that crossed the snow bank near the tent until he fell asleep and dreamed the strangest dream. In it the wolves, like the whales and dolphins, were speaking in a language that humans, with the help of their recorders and computers, had finally learned to understand.

Just as he overheard what the first wolf said to the second wolf and translated it into English, Matthew woke up with a sudden start. It must be morning. He cautiously unzipped the tent flap and, looking out, saw the last long wisps of fog go drifting out to sea. The wolves had vanished.

After they had eaten, Kayak went with Matt, who was following his father. They watched Ross Morgan as he crouched behind one of the stone men, sighting along its arm.

"Charlie," he shouted, "will you go and hold this rifle upright over there? Move the rifle barrel a little to the right," he called as though he were an engineer surveying a new road. "More! More! There—hold it!"

Mr. Morgan walked to another stone man, and then another, each time bending and sighting carefully along the *inukshuk*'s outstretched arm.

"All of these stone men are pointing west—directly at that rifle barrel," he exclaimed. "Only those three largest statues standing over there are pointing north, as though they were trying to show us the way to some other place."

"That's what my grandfather told me," Kayak said, as he, too, looked along the stone men's arms. "All these *inukshuks* are pointing to a tip of land that's too far west for us to see. We call it Sharlo. My teacher says the English explorers named it Sea Horse Point on their maps. That's on Southampton Island. Long ago our women used to row over there in their big skin *umiaks* piled high with tents and meat, grandparents, children, dogs and even sleds. Of course, our hunters went along with them, but they were paddling in their kayaks. Because of the long distance and the danger of storms, they used to gather first in this place and use these pointing stone men to guide them by the shortest route."

"What did your grandfather say about these three larger stone men pointing north?" Matthew's father asked.

"He said those are a lot older than the others. Tunik people built them so they pointed toward *Inuk-shuk-sha-lik-juak*. It's supposed to be far north of here, a land our people used to know in very ancient times. Perhaps it was just a dream."

"It sounds like a fairy tale to me." Charlie laughed. "My grandmother used to tell me old stories when I visited her in Alice Springs—about magic islands, caves with dwarfs and giants, and unicorns and mountain kings."

"We're supposed to be out here searching for gold

and not for fairy stories." Mr. Morgan snorted. "If we don't find it soon, I'll end up in the poor house, and you'll see Charlie earn his living shoveling snow next winter."

"Not ruddy likely!" Charlie chuckled. "If our gold scheme fails, I'll get an Australian soldier's shade hat and a good-sized water bottle on my hip. Me and Matilda will be heading for the desert outback. I've got a liking for Dajarra—that's in Queensland. You can find it on some maps. It's nice and warm up there and not what you'd call overcrowded."

"Meanwhile, Charlie says he's got to do some work on Matilda's engine," Matt's father said, "and I want to study these maps. Would you two like to go up on that small hill with my binoculars? See if you can see land to the north or west."

As Matt and Kayak started up the long sloping hillside, they could see patches of purple fireweed and white Arctic cotton and beyond that small Alpine star flowers and bright yellow poppies waving in the pleasant summer breezes that blew in from the south.

Kayak said, "My teacher told me we got very old trees growing right here in our tundra just like you've got in Arizooona or Ontariooo. Only she says our trees are kind of small."

Kayak knelt down and showed Matt a tiny twisted dwarf willow near a birch tree. They were each only one inch high. Matthew could see that they were fully grown and formed like trees, but these dwarfed trees leaned sideways on top of the ground. Bent by the Arctic winds, they hugged the earth in cracks between the rocks, staying small but very much alive.

Kayak and Matt lay on the hill and searched the far horizons of the sea. But they saw nothing. Matthew moved the binoculars until he glimpsed the flash of Matilda's bright red side.

"I can see Charlie's working on Matilda's engine," Matt said. He slowly eased his line of sight past the helicopter toward the tent. He stopped, then shouted at his father who was getting water at the stream, too far away to hear him.

"Look, quick!" he gasped, handing Kayak the binoculars. "There's a huge white polar bear! And Charlie hasn't seen it."

"I don't see any . . . oh, yes I do," Kayak replied. "It's a really big one, coming up behind him." He swung the binoculars back on Charlie. "He's going right on working. He doesn't know that bear is sneaking up on him."

Matthew cupped his hands and shouted, "CHARLIE! CHARLIE! WATCH OUT BEHIND YOU! THERE'S A BEAR!"

"That won't do any good," said Kayak. "The wind's against you and he's far away, more than half a mile. He won't hear you."

"What are we going to do?" cried Matthew. "Can we run down there and warn him in time?"

Kayak jumped up. "He's too far away. That bear is almost on top of him."

Kayak handed Matthew the binoculars, then dug into his shirt pocket underneath his parka and pulled out his knife and the neat black plastic case, containing a mirror, that his girl friend had given him. With his knife point he scratched a bare spot in the mercury on the back of the mirror. Using the bare spot like a gun sight, he lined up the small mirror with the sun, then sighted on Matilda.

Matthew, watching with the binoculars, suddenly saw a small signal of bright light run across the rock until it reached the bear. The animal stopped and looked up at the nervous jumping patch of light flashed by Kayak's mirror.

"Shine it on Charlie," Matthew called to Kayak.

He held his breath and watched as the tiny square of light went running once more toward the helicopter and played along its bright red side.

"Poor Charlie!" Kayak yelled in frustration. "He's got his head inside the engine covering. He's never going to see that light."

"Look at the bear," screamed Matthew. "It's close enough to touch Charlie and still he doesn't know it's there!"

"Try the pool. Flash it on the pool of water near Charlie's feet," cried Matthew.

When Kayak did that, the double reflection of the light must have glanced up into Charlie's eyes. He immediately withdrew his head from beneath Matilda's engine cover and looked up toward the source of the distant flashing mirror.

Quickly Kayak shifted the light from the pool at Charlie's feet back onto the bear's eyes, trying to confuse it. But it was too late. The monstrous white beast was almost on top of Charlie. It began to move in to attack.

"Charlie's turning around. He's seen the bear," yelled Matthew. He kept the big field glasses trained on Charlie, who pulled off Matilda's bright red engine cowling just in time and swung it in front of him like a shield. Matthew shouted with excitement when he saw the bear reach out with one of its huge paws and strike the metal cover. "The bear almost knocked Charlie down," he yelled to Kayak. "Now Charlie's running and the bear is right behind him. They're both running round and round Matilda. The bear is gaining on him. There—Charlie's stopped! Hurry, Charlie, hurry. There—he's jerked Matilda's door open. But he can't get in! The bear is too close. Look, Charlie's running round again! The door is open. The bear is gaining fast. He's jumping in."

"Who's jumping in?" yelled Kayak.

"Charlie's jumping in. The bear is trying hard to climb in after him. Charlie's trying to close Matilda's door. Good work, Charlie! Good for you! He's trying to slam it, but . . . but wait . . . the bear has one paw inside the door. I can see through Matilda's bubble window. Charlie's doing something to the bear. The bear's lunging away from Charlie. It's pulling its paw out of Matilda's door. It's doing it very fast! The bear's mouth is wide open. It must be roaring. Now it's running away. And Charlie, he's sitting safe inside the helicopter with the door tight shut. I think he's laughing."

"Phew!" said Kayak. "Let me borrow those binoculars. I can't believe we made it work."

"You made it work, all right," Matthew replied. "You probably saved Charlie's life with that small mirror. What made you think of that trick?"

"I learned it from you," Kayak said, "Remember? You told me once it was an Apache Indian way of signaling in Arizooona. I thought that was a good idea."

Matthew saw his father running up toward them from the stream. "Say, you two. What's all the shouting about? Have you sighted land out there?"

"No," said Kayak. "We were not yelling about land. We were calling to warn Charlie. He was being hunted by a big white bear."

"A *bear*? Where is it now? Where is Charlie?"

"The bear's run away. Charlie's safe inside the helicopter," Matthew said.

"Let's get down there and make certain he's all right," said Mr. Morgan.

They hurried down over the gray sloping granite rocks until they came within easy shouting distance of Matilda.

Matthew's father stopped, cupped his hands around

his mouth and bellowed, "Where's the bear?"

"He went to cool off with a swim," yelled Charlie, and he pointed out to sea.

When they reached Matilda, Charlie had the door wide open and they could hear him singing in his heartiest voice:

> "Waltzing Matilda,
> Waltzing Matilda,
> I'll come awaltzing Matilda
> With you."

"I watched you with the binoculars," Matthew said. "When that bear reached inside Matilda, what did you do that made it roar and run away?"

"That's the great Australian secret, laddos." Charlie raised one foot and held out his powerful calloused hand toward Matthew and then Kayak. "I can't explain to you exactly how it's done, but I shall gladly give you both a firsthand demonstration. It's called the kangaroo kickback."

"You first?" Kayak said to Matthew.

"No, thank you, not today! I'll let Kayak be first."

"I'll be glad to learn the kangaroo kickback," said Kayak, "but not until I'm bigger than a polar bear."

They took down their camp and packed up their equipment.

"We're off," said Mr. Morgan, "to wherever those three stone men are pointing. I wonder if Inuit have ever lived there?"

They flew north over Foxe Basin. Matthew looked down in wonder at the slowly moving jigsaw puzzle of broken sea ice drifting southward to melt in Hudson Bay.

"According to my map, we're heading to Prince Charles Island," Mr. Morgan said in a few minutes. "That's just west of Baffin Island. I suppose the Eskimos could have crossed over long ago in the winter by dog team or they might have come by boat in summer."

"There's land ahead!" said Charlie.

As Matilda whirled in over the south end of the enormous island, Charlie shouted, "Where do you want me to set her down?"

"There's a good place," Ross Morgan said. "I think I see one more of those big stone men down there."

Charlie landed Matilda on a little knoll. Matt and Kayak jumped out and followed Mr. Morgan toward the largest *inukshuk* they had seen yet, much taller than an ordinary man.

"This place must be *Inuk-shuk-sha-lik-juak*," Kayak said. "See how this statue has been built in a very different way—with its stone legs spread wide apart." He stood on his tiptoes to sight along its outstretched arm. "It is pointing at that low gray cliff ahead of us."

"It's hard to believe these maps," said Matthew's father as he smoothed them out with his hand. "Prince Charles Island is immense. Do you boys realize that this one island that we're standing on is over eight thousand square miles in size and yet no one even knew of its existence until some time around 1950 when an Air Force photo reconnaissance plane flew over in the summer and recorded it for the first time? That caused a great stir among geographers around the world. Imagine us finding such an enormous island so recently, after we thought we had discovered everything. The moving ice and dangerous tides make this one of the most difficult places to reach on the face of this globe."

After they had set up the two red tents on a gravel knoll safely away from the damp tundra and some distance from Matilda, Matt's father said, "I'm not going to miss this chance to search this island over. There may be rich metal deposits. We should stay here for a while."

Matt looked around. It was strange—like making camp for the first time on the face of the moon.

"Fine," said Charlie. "But if we're going to fly around here searching for metal, Matilda will drink up lots of gasoline. I'll have to go back to Mingo and ferry some up here while the weather's good." Charlie rubbed his bad leg and added, "But I can't roll a gas drum up into Matilda by myself. Would you two laddos mind being left alone again?"

"We'll be all right," Matthew said, looking at Kayak, "if you and Dad are away no longer than you were the last time."

Charlie squinted up at the Arctic sun and said,

"If we're going, let's go now. Around here it's best to do things while the weather's right."

"Just one thing," said Matthew. "When you go up, would you mind circling around once to look for polar bears?"

"Sure, we'll do that," said Charlie.

Kayak and Matt walked down and watched the two men climb aboard Matilda.

"We should be back tomorrow with all the gasoline that she will carry," said Matt's father. "We left the rifle in your tent, and almost everything else you'll need is there, too."

"Remember, laddos," Charlie added "leave a note for us if you go off to see the sights."

Kayak looked up at the sky, then glanced at Charlie.

"Stop worrying." Charlie laughed. "The weather's going to be just fine. Keep your eyes open for any roving polar bears. You both know how to use the rifle."

Matilda's engine roared into life and her huge blades spun silver patterns in the air. She hovered just above them.

"I hope they don't get lost again," said Matthew, as they waved and then watched the helicopter grow mosquito small and disappear into the eastern sky. "I feel kind of lonely already."

They listened to the awesome Arctic silence, then turned and walked back up the slope toward the tents.

"Wait! Don't go any closer," Kayak whispered, and he clutched Matt's arm.

Even as he spoke they could see the red nylon sides of their tent twitch and turn, then bulge out full.

"Oh," Matthew groaned in terror. "There's something huge inside."

VIII

CURIOUS RAINBOWS

"THE RIFLE'S IN THE TENT," MATT WHISPERED, "AND there's no way of getting it now."

"Crouch down behind that rock," said Kayak. Then he yelled toward the tent as fiercely as he could and ducked out of sight, too.

All movement in the tent stopped at the sound of Kayak's voice. The boys waited, silently. Suddenly they saw violent motions pushing out the sides of the tent again as if a dozen fists and heads and rumps and elbows were thrashing against the soft red nylon walls.

"What's going on in there?" yelled Matthew.

As if to answer him, a short, hairy white figure leaped outside the tent. Standing upright, it peered inside again, watching the commotion until it was joined by another figure.

"I told you we should always zipper that tent tight." Kayak gave a relieved laugh.

"Are they ghosts?" asked Matthew. "Or are they the wild man's children?"

"No, not ghosts." Kayak chuckled. "They're *okalik*, big white Arctic hares. Our tent is full of them."

As he spoke, another half-dozen pure white hares hopped out of the tent and in a moment they were followed by five more. Each one of them stood more than two feet high.

"They won't hurt us," Kayak said. "Get up so they can see you."

Matt felt foolish, as he rose from his hiding place behind the rock. The big hares crowded together, staring at the two boys curiously. They stood on tiptoes with their short ears cocked up, listening. Four more big ones came hopping out of the tent to join the others.

"Fifteen, sixteen, seventeen of them," Kayak counted. "I've heard about them flocking together like that, but I never thought I'd see them do it. My father says *okalik* only do that on the loneliest islands."

The hares must have heard Kayak speak, for they all laid back their ears and still standing on their hind feet, close packed together, went hopping and skipping away across the tundra until they disappeared behind a gravel ridge.

"That was like looking at a picture out of *Alice In*

Wonderland," said Matthew. "Imagine all those white rabbits running around upright like humans. What were they doing in our tent?"

"I don't know," said Kayak. "They're curious about us, I guess. They probably thought our red tent might be a lovely place to live. Remember, Mattoosie, all the animals are different out here. They don't know that they're supposed to run on four feet and be afraid of humans."

"I'm sorry that they've gone," said Matthew. "It was good to have some company."

"You won't like it so much when you look inside our tent and see how those *okalik* have been poking into everything."

"Phew!" said Matthew after they'd gone in. "It looks like a chocolate drop factory!"

When they had tidied the tent, Matthew stepped outside and said, "Won't the wind bother us up here on this hill?"

"Yes, it will," said Kayak. "That's why we'll have to weight our tent down all round with heavy rocks. But what we want most is dry ground underneath our sleeping bags even when it's raining hard and that's why this is a good place to stay. That's the way the Tuniks used to do it."

"Are you sure Tuniks lived here?" Matthew asked him.

"Yes," said Kayak. "See those shallow holes in the tundra with all the tumbled stones? Those are the ruins of their old houses. My grandfather told me that they were short people, but very, very strong. Lots of people say that there are still some Tunik people living in our country on the far-off islands and up the hidden mountain fiords where our hunters seldom go."

Kayak pointed. "Over there you can see where the Tuniks used to play a favorite game of theirs. In that long narrow sand pit there are big round stones at either end. Two strong men each used to pick up a heavy boulder and see who could shuffle fastest through the deep sand. That's really hard to do. Let's try it."

Matthew and Kayak together attempted to heave one of the heavy stones. They could scarcely move it.

"If we lived among the Tunik people, we'd never get a wife," Kayak remarked. "They say Tunik girls wouldn't marry a young hunter unless he could run up and down the sand pit carrying a heavy rock like that to prove himself to them."

Kayak stared at the moss-covered house ruins. "I wish we could have found some of those strong Tunik people still living here. I'd like to have talked to them about how life used to be."

Matthew looked at the circles of stones and said, "They must have had three, four, five skin tents pitched—here on the highest ground." Then he laughed and added, "I feel just like Christopher Columbus discovering this island, even though I guess your people were here much earlier."

Kayak smiled and said, "I'm a little bit like you,

Mattoosie. I feel like Christy-for-Cooloomboos, too!"

Kayak took a long, heavy knife from the pack and a tin of meat. "Mattoosie, you want half of this?" he asked.

"Sure," said Matthew, who watched in surprise as Kayak turned the metal can on its side and neatly sliced it into two halves.

Kayak handed Matt one half and kept the other one himself.

"That's a funny way to do it," Matthew said.

"A good way," said Kayak. "We both got exactly half and a nice tin to eat it from."

They shared some hardtack biscuits and dried prunes.

"You want to make some tea?" asked Matthew.

"Yes," said Kayak. "I'll make it," and he went outside the tent and dipped some cold, clear water from a nearby stream into their kettle.

Between their sleeping bags, Matthew put down with care the unloaded rifle and placed the bullets close beside it. Kayak and Matthew slept peacefully until dawn when flight after flight of geese came in honking low over their tent.

"We could take one or two of them easily," said Kayak, "but we don't have to now. We have other food to eat. Every one of those geese has a mate, now that summer's here. I hate to kill a goose husband or a goose wife and leave the other one lonely and calling for its mate."

"I know how that is," Matthew said, as he thought of his own family.

"I need some tea," said Kayak. "You can see your breath in here this morning."

He opened an air space in the tent flap, then pumped up the small brass primus stove and put the kettle on to heat. They ate another hardtack biscuit and a spoonful of honey and drank the good hot tea.

"Phew, it's getting warm in here," said Kayak, as he unzipped their tent flap all the way.

There were so many white geese on the tundra slope that at first Matthew thought he was looking at a field of snow that waddled.

When Kayak and Matt stepped out of the tent, they heard the guardian ganders honking out the danger signal. Geese rose in the thousands, circled, and then flew on north to build their nests in the summer tundra.

"I can't tell you exactly why," said Matthew, "but I like this lonely island more than almost any place I've ever been."

Kayak reached into his pocket and took out the small mirror his girl friend had sent him from King-merok where she lived. He glanced at himself in it and said, "Mattoosie, wasn't my *nuliungasak*—that means material for a wife—wasn't she nice to send me this? When we get married, we will build our own igloo in the winter and tent together in the summer. I'll hunt hard for her and she'll sew my boots and make harpoon line for me. With her, I'll be able to travel and hunt anywhere"—he spread his arms—"in this whole country."

"She calls me *uingasak*. That means I'm material to be her husband. I sent word to her about you, Mattoosie. My cousin told her you were my adopted brother. If you want to, you can come and live with us. She probably won't mind making the boots for you, too. Or maybe by then you'll have a wife, and we can all four make a winter camp together."

"I never thought of anything like that," said Matthew. "But I've never really thought about having a wife. I mean, I wonder how she'll look. I wonder what she'll have to say? Imagine me with a wife!"

"I'll let you know what mine says soon," said Kayak. "The day her family agrees that I can go and stay with them, I'm going! But now, let's go walking," Kayak said. "Let's go and leave our footprints on this island."

Except for the low gray stone hill that stood before them Prince Charles Island was largely flat. Beyond the hill they could see a wide, shallow lake and around it broad stretches of grey-green caribou moss growing in the tundra, which was also spotted with countless summer flowers. Snowbirds flew about in small nervous flocks. The male ptarmigan called, *"Come here, come here,"* across the wide open spaces of the tundra and were answered by the females who called back, *"Geta-bible, geta-bible."*

"I've never been in such a lonely place surrounded by all of nature," Matthew said, as he picked low growing lingonberries and stuffed them in his mouth.

As if in answer, Kayak said, "I'm going to lie down here on this sun-warmed gravel. You lie down, Mattoosie, too. Don't speak one word. Just look around the land and up at the sky and think how lucky we are to have this beautiful island all to ourselves."

After a long silence, Matthew spoke "It's wonderful. It's like a magic place. Dad and Charlie are the only ones who know we're here."

"There's someone sitting over there who knows you're here," said Kayak, "and she doesn't like it very much."

Kayak pulled his parka hood over his head as a snowy owl rose sharply from her nest on the open tundra, her claws hooked dangerously as she flew toward them.

"Look, there are her young sitting in a nest on the flat ground," said Matthew, and he moved in closer to have a better look.

"You be careful," Kayak warned him, as the owl turned and swooped at Matthew, beating her wide white wings.

Matthew dodged and bent over just as the female owl spread her tail and plunged down, snatching with her claws at his back. He felt her curved black talons tear his eiderdown parka, sending the soft gray down fluttering out along the north wind's path.

"She's getting mad," said Kayak. "You come away from her young ones, or she'll tear at you twice as hard. She won't give up."

Still bending, Matthew ran, saying, "Maybe she's the same owl that showed us the gold locked in the ice."

"I don't think so," Kayak replied. "Most snowy owls act like that, if you go too near their nests. They guard their young."

Together they hurried up the long slope, away from the nest, toward the gray stone hill.

"Do you think we'll find gold out here?" Kayak asked him.

"I doubt it," Matthew said. "The gray shale rocks on this island don't look right for gold. That may be why the wild man led us here, to get us away from where the gold really is."

"He is cunning," Kayak said. "I think he pulled the old broken wing trick on us."

"What do you mean, the broken wing trick?" Matthew asked.

"Have you not noticed," Kayak said, "the way ducks and shore birds act? If you go near them, they protect their young by fluttering along the water or over the ground. They pretend they have a broken wing until the man or fox or hawk starts chasing after them. These birds keep just ahead of their pursuers, trying to lead them from their young. That's exactly what I think the wild man did to us.

He led us away from his secret home beside the golden river."

"You may be right," said Matthew. "We were kind of crazy maybe to trail across Baffin Island following those pointing stone men."

"And yet"—Kayak laughed—"we are doing the same thing right now. Following that big *inukshuk* because it's aiming its arm toward that hill in front of us."

"We've come this far, we might as well go all the way," Matthew answered.

"Wait! Don't go any farther," said Kayak. "I want you to look down into that pool beside your feet. What do you see?" he asked.

"Rainbows," said Matthew. "I see wonderful rainbows of the brightest hues: bands of red, yellow, green and blue."

Kayak drew in his breath and said in an excited voice, "Mattoosie, our teacher said that could mean *oil!*"

"Oh, no. Lot's of people have been fooled by that before," Matt said. "That's mosquito larvae. Mosquitoes are born into the water in tiny oily sacks. That's what makes this stagnant water glisten just like a pool of oil. They must be hatching out."

"Mattoosie, are you sure?" Kayak asked him. "I been looking at thin oil on mosquito waters all my life, but this"—he pointed with his finger—"this oily water looks heavy like it fell out of an army oil truck."

"That's because—as everyone says—you've got bigger, stronger mosquitoes living in the north! Of course, big bugs like that need richer, thicker oil," Matthew replied.

Kayak bent down and took some of the oil up on his fingers. He smelled it carefully, then held his hand beneath Matthew's nose.

"What's that smell like?" Kayak asked him.

"Matilda when she's taking off in the early morning," Matthew replied.

"That's right. That's why Charlie was working on her engine. He said she was burning oil."

"My father and Charlie are so eager to find something they can stake as a claim that they've got you thinking that even these mosquitoes are sucking oil. Well, they're not. They're having young. They'll be hatched out and chasing us across the tundra by tomorrow evening. Just you wait and see."

Since they were hungry and there was plenty of time to explore the hill they'd been heading for, they turned back to the tents, ate again and went to sleep. In the morning, Matthew's watch had stopped.

"I wonder how long we've slept?" he asked. "It may be six o'clock in the morning or six o'clock at night but we can't tell because it's light all the time."

"Mattoosie, eat when you're hungry," Kayak said, "sleep when you're tired. Don't worry about the time. That's the way my people do it."

"Listen!" said Matthew. "I hear Matilda! She's coming back—she's almost here!"

Matilda hovered near their tents and nearly blew them over as she landed.

"It's good to see you both again," Matt's father called to them. "You want to help us offload these drums of gasoline?"

"Handle with care, my buckos. Gas fires are the very worst of all," warned Charlie.

While Charlie was cooking a breakfast of his famous banger sausages Australian outback style, Matt's father said, "Did you boys see anything interesting?"

"Not really," Matthew answered.

"I think we did," said Kayak. "Where that *inukshuk* is pointing, we found some oil spread in a shallow pool. It smelled just like Matilda. I think it's coming up out of the rocks."

"It was mosquito larvae," Matthew said.

"What are you two laddos nattering about?" asked Charlie.

"When you're finished eating those delicious bangers," Kayak said, "we'll walk over there and show you."

"You don't need to be in too much of a hurry, Charlie," Matthew said. "You've probably seen mosquito larvae lots of times before."

When they reached the pool, Matthew's father and Charlie squatted down and silently examined the reflecting rainbow glow.

"What do you think?" said Charlie, looking Mr. Morgan in the eye.

"I really don't know," Ross Morgan answered, and he squatted down and sniffed. "As Matt says, it could be mosquito larvae and as Kayak says, it just might be something much, much better."

"How are we going to judge a thing like that?" asked Charlie. "I mean, you're some kind of a hard rock expert. You didn't do your prospecting in oil or natural gas."

"You're right," said Matthew's father. "I'm certainly no wildcat oilman. I don't know a thing about it. Real oil men know how to assay salt domes, judge the depths of shale basins and potential paying wells. But I can tell you this—that one of the most important oil strikes ever found in Canada was by a cowboy, they said, knew even less that I do. That was in southern Alberta."

"How did he do that?" asked Charlie.

"I heard," said Ross Morgan, "that this cowboy saw something like a rainbow slick shining in a slough. He leaned on his saddle horn just staring at it for a while and then he took a match out of his pocket, struck it on his thumbnail and chucked it out in front of him."

"What happened?" Charlie asked.

"The whole damn slough blew up into roaring flames and singed most of the hair off both the cowboy and his horse! The province of Alberta started getting richer and more famous from that day to this!"

"What does that mean to us?" asked Charlie.

"Well," said Mr. Morgan, and he reached into his pocket. "It's an old fashioned cowboy trick and it's not very scientific." He struck a match. "But I'm going to try it. Stand back upwind, boys. Here goes!"

He tossed the lighted match toward the long stone crack beside the rainbow pool.

IX

ISLAND EXPLORERS

THERE WAS A VIOLENT PUFF OF ORANGE AS FLAMES raced across the shallow pool, fanned by the west wind, and black smoke billowed out toward the sea ice.

"Leaping lizards!" shouted Charlie.

"Holy smoke!" gasped Matt's father.

"It's oil! Real oil!" screamed Kayak.

"I admit," yelled Matthew, "mosquito larvae wouldn't burn like that."

"You're right." Mr. Morgan laughed as he clapped his big rough hand around Matt's shoulders. "You're staring at our fame and fortune, not in copper, nor in gold, but real black diamonds—that's what the oil men call it. I'll bet we're standing on a vast oil deposit loaded with natural gas as well. At the very moment when the whole world needs energy, we four have found it"—he snapped his fingers—"just like that!"

"Matt, run back to the tent and bring me Matilda's emergency paddle. I don't want to stand too close, but I want to stir up this pool. The water underneath should easily snuff out this small fire, unless it's highly concentrated oil, and, believe me, I hope and pray it is! I hope there's a billion barrels of rich crude and many trillion cubic feet of natural gas lying underneath our feet."

Matthew hurried back with the paddle and watched as his father carefully stirred the pool. The flames increased and billowed with black smoke.

"Wonderful!" his father said.

"It's coming up from way down under," Charlie said and danced an outback jig beside the fire. "It burns like pure oil," he yelled. "Looks like we've struck it rich."

Matt's father gave a violent sweep across the pool and snuffed out all the flames.

"Good," he said. "We don't want to waste our precious treasure." He looked around him. "There may be other pools near here that show signs of oil, or rock cracks that are seeping natural gas. You two boys might go out and have a look around for us. Charlie and I are going to stay here, gather some samples and build up a stone cairn to mark this find of ours. Matt," his father shouted, "don't light any matches!"

Kayak and Matthew shouldered their light packs and started off across the country.

Matthew let out his breath in a whistle. "I couldn't believe my eyes when that rainbow pool caught fire. It proved you were right. There certainly wasn't much water there."

As the Arctic sun dipped down into the western sea, Kayak sat on the tundra and examined the holes he had worn through his sealskin boot soles. "It's no good living far away from women," Kayak said. "When Charlie flies back to Frobisher, I'm going to send a letter written in *Inuktitut* to my mother and my grandmother, asking them to make us both some new skin boots. I only have one more pair. When the snow starts flying, I don't want to be out here in my bare feet."

Matthew leaned against a rock and, using the binoculars, examined the pools of water that lay to the north and east of them.

"That may be more oil over there," he said. They rose and hurried toward it.

"Dad and Charlie are going to do a dance when they hear that we've found more pools of oil," Matt said a little later.

They paused and rested on their packs and ate their canned meat on hardtack biscuits. Because it was soft on the tundra and the sun was warm, they both fell sound asleep.

❀ ❀ ❀

Later, they ate their evening meal with Charlie and Mr. Morgan outside the two red tents.

Matt's father said, "There has been oil lying under these rocks and snow for million of years just waiting to be found. When you look out over this treeless Arctic island, can you imagine that all this was once covered with lush green swamplands and strange thick trees that looked like huge pineapples? Enormous dinosaurs roamed these northern islands millions of years ago when the climate here was steaming hot. Long-necked brontosaurs battled with the deadly tyrannosaurus rex, while those leather-winged monsters, pterosaurs, soared above their heads. Slowly this northern world changed as the climate cooled, and all those curious trees and ancient animals fell into the swamps and slowly sank away to become coal and oil and natural gas, all precious gifts of fossil fuel from an age long before mankind existed."

"Our teacher told us," Kayak said, "that oil is a gift to all of us, not at all like the meat of caribou or fish or even people who may be grown again. Once the oil and coal and gas are taken out of the earth and used, they will never reappear again."

"Exactly right," said Matt's father. "I've been thinking about what we should do now," he continued. "What I suggest will take some time. But I think it will be more than worth it in the end. First, I believe that we should go and find Professor Volks."

"Professor Volks?" said Charlie. "He's famous! But

how are we ever going to find him?" He laughed. "We're here on a remote island in the Arctic Archipelago and Professor Volks may be in Scandinavia, or Africa, or central China, helping them find oil. I think it would be easier to fly Matilda upside down or to shake hands with a polar bear than find Professor Volks."

"I read in the *Northern Miner* that he was going to be lecturing at some universities in the United States and Canada. I'll bet that we can find him," Matthew's father said. "We need Professor Volks. He knows more about oil discovery than any other person in the world."

"Would you boys mind if you had to wait here for a while for us? Somebody's got to guard our oil claim until we get it registered with the government."

"You go and get him," Kayak said. "I want to see a man like that."

"Yes, you go," said Matthew. "We'll take care of ourselves." But as he spoke he was thinking of his mother, of their thin-walled nylon tent and of the enormous polar bear that had come so close to Charlie. His father was the only family he had left. He spoke again slowly. "Yes, it's all right if you go . . . but . . . but come back as soon as you can."

Kayak reached into the flour sack inside his sleeping roll and drew out the heavy golden dagger. Its long yellow blade glinted in the evening sunlight.

"This isn't mine," he said. "It belongs to all of us."

"It's beautiful," said Matthew's father. "Look at

the way someone has carefully beaten and turned the hilt into those handsome double curves."

"A knife like that," said Charlie, "must be worth an awful lot of money."

"Yes, it is," said Matthew's father as he weighed it in his hand. "That much gold melted down would pay off all of Matilda's repairs and all our debt for gasoline and more."

"To get money would they have to melt that dagger down?" asked Kayak.

"A gold treasure like that belongs in a museum," said Matthew. "We'd tell them that they're not allowed to melt it down."

"Why don't we sort of loan that knife?" said Kayak. "I mean to pay for Matilda so they won't have to chase Charlie down the runway when he returns to Frobisher. Let's tell them that we only loan them our yellow knife and later when this rich mosquito oil starts pumping up for all of us, we'll use that money to pay for Matilda's parts, then buy the golden dagger back and put it into a museum where everyone can see it."

"Good thinking," Charlie said.

"It's up to you two boys. Do you really want to do it that way?" Mr. Morgan asked them.

"It's the best way," Kayak said, and Matthew nodded in agreement.

"I'll give the knife to them," said Charlie, "through the Mounted Police at Frobisher. The constable will be a witness. They will sign a paper, and then the knife will be kept in the police safe until it goes to a museum."

Charlie laid the heavy golden knife in a leather case among his maps and flight plans.

In the early morning, the two men unloaded the last things from Matilda and prepared for takeoff.

"Good luck." Matt's father shook hands with his son and Kayak and handed them an extra box of ammunition for the rifle. "We won't be gone too long, I hope. You have plenty of supplies."

"Pip, pip, laddos," Charlie called to them.

Matthew and Kayak pulled up their parka hoods as they felt the churning wind from the propellers. Matilda rose into the air. Matt's father and Charlie waved good-by as the helicopter turned and whirled away, disappearing into the glare of the rising sun.

"I hate to see them go," said Matthew.

"So do I," said Kayak.

"What I minded most was the handshake and the serious look on my dad's face as though he wasn't sure if he'd see either of us again."

Two whole weeks passed and there was not a sight or sound of human life, except for themselves. Their food rations were getting low.

"It's cold out there this morning." Matthew shivered. "I wonder where they are?" He thought of the warm Pacific breezes blowing over the coast of Peru.

Kayak sniffed the air and turning, looked at the heavy cloud banks forming over Foxe Channel. "I think today is going to be the day for really heavy snow to come."

And so it did—hard driving snow, turning to a violent autumn blizzard that threatened to tear to pieces the thin fabric of the tent that protected them. When Matthew woke, the red west wall of their tent bulged inward, the snow piled up outside pressing it down against his sleeping bag.

"We're going to have to dig our way out of here," said Kayak. "That's not going to be so easy. Autumn snow is often wet and it can weigh like lead. I wish we had a shovel."

"We've got one," Matthew said, "if I can get my hand underneath this tent without getting out of my sleeping bag. I think I know just where it is."

He reached beneath the edge flap near the entrance and pulled in a little folded piece of iron and wood.

"What's that?" asked Kayak.

"It's a small shovel," Matthew said, as he fitted it together. "It's the kind soldiers used to use to dig fox holes in the ground when they were fighting."

"The shovel's a good idea," said Kayak, "but the idea of men fighting each other is a really bad idea. Why do people do it?"

Matthew thought about that for some time and then said, "I don't know exactly why they do it. It's usually about somebody taking somebody else's land."

"Land should belong to everyone," said Kayak, "like the sun and moon and stars and the ocean and the lakes and rivers. I would never fight with you, Mattoosie. I hate the idea of humans fighting with each other."

"Do you mean," said Matthew, "that if I came bursting into your house with a knife in my hand and tried to kill your mother or your sister you wouldn't fight me?"

"That's different! Then I would fight you hard!" Kayak said, and for the first time Matt saw a fierce and angry look come over Kayak's face. "I'd stop you. Yes, I'd have to stop you, any way I could."

"That's what war is about, I guess," said Matthew. "It's bad, it's terrible, but sometimes it can't be helped."

"Let me reach out of my sleeping bag and unzip this tent flap," Matthew went on, "and we'll both fight against the weather."

"Just when we think the white people are kind of crazy," said Kayak, "they show us a wonderful little shovel like this one. I'll do the digging," he said, and started energetically throwing the snow back toward Matthew's head. Some went into his sleeping bag.

"I guess that's a hint that it's time for me to get up." Matthew laughed as he jumped out of the bag.

Taking turns with the shovel, they dug a tunnel and finally stood upright in their new exit, gasping, staring at the harshly glaring world of snow that now spread over Prince Charles Island. The coal-black winter sea around the island looked bleakly cold. It was as though the water had become thick as icy syrup and now lay waiting to be frozen solid.

"I'm glad we set up the four stone markers to show us where the oil seeps are," said Matthew. He pointed at the big *inukshuk* near their tent. "Even that stone man looks like a friend to me. Snow makes this island seem more lonely."

"You better get used to it," Kayak warned. "It's going to stay this way until summer comes next year. Cheer up! It's October! If we weren't here, we'd be back in school this morning."

Matt cut two pieces of leather from the map case and made himself a pair of insoles for his worn out sealskin boots. Kayak would need to patch his soon, too. Matt looked to the east above the flat horizon, hoping he might see or hear Matilda, but saw only somber white against the skull-shaped island stones. A lean black raven winged its way across the sky, cawing as it tried to break the silence of the coming winter.

Once when they went walking, they crossed the huge pad prints of a polar bear. After that they carried the rifle.

Matilda had been gone for seventeen days and the moon was coming full again when they discovered the tracks of a dozen caribou. But though they followed the trail for miles, they never saw one. On the eighteenth night, there was a great display of northern lights moving among the stars above their heads.

Next day, the temperature plunged downward. The salt water round the island steamed with fog and formed small ice pans near the shore.

They watched the sky in the southeast day after day, hoping that they would hear and see Matilda. But she did not come.

"I'm really getting worried about my dad and Charlie," Matthew said. "They should be back by now. We'll be starving, if they don't come soon. Our food is getting short. We've only two tins of meat, six packages of dried soup and half a box of apricots.

"*Ionamut*," said Kayak. "We can't help that. We can't change the way things are going to happen."

On the following morning, Kayak unzipped the tent. "Look over there," he whispered, pointing at the hill.

"I don't see anything," Matt said, as he peered out of their tent across the glaring snow.

"Tell me," said Kayak, "will that wooden shovel handle come off?"

"Yes, it comes apart into three pieces," Matt answered.

"Good. Give me the handle and stay close behind me so they won't see you."

"Who won't see me?" Matt snorted. "There's nothing alive out there."

"Come on," Kayak whispered, and crouching low, he moved quickly toward the hill.

When they paused for a moment, Kayak pointed

again and said, "*Akigik.*"

Only then did Matt see one, three, six, eight, ten, more than twenty snow-white ptarmigan in a flock strutting nervously before them. These plump birds the size of small chickens moved on thickly feathered legs and feet.

"We should have brought the rifle," Matthew said.

"Too noisy," Kayak answered.

Saying that, he drew back his hand and with a flick of his wrist sent the shovel handle whirling flat like a helicopter's blades just a hand's width above the snow. It struck silently into the very center of the white birds and Matt saw three of them knocked senseless.

The other ptarmigan flew a short distance, then landed. Kayak hurried forward and grasped the handle.

"You pick up those three birds and follow me." Matt watched Kayak bend and send the handle whirling toward the ptarmigan again. Two more were stunned.

"You want to try it?" Kayak whispered.

"No, I see you know just how to do it."

After the next throw Kayak said, "That's enough," as Matt picked up the ninth white bird.

"I'm really hungry," Matt said.

"First we got to thank the spirit of those birds," said Kayak, "for giving us their flesh to eat." He carefully plucked tail feathers from each one of the white birds and stood them upright in the snow. "*Nakoami-asit*. Thanks a lot," he called into the west where the flock of ptarmigan had flown.

That evening in the tent they plucked, boiled and ate two of the birds, then drank the rich, thick broth. Matt told Kayak he had never tasted anything so fine in all his life.

"When your belly's full, your worries seem to fly away." Kayak sighed as he lay back in his sleeping bag. "I'd like to hunt birds with those Indians you know in Arizooona. I wonder how they do it?"

Next day to occupy their time Kayak took Matt exploring along the low cliff. He picked here and there with his knife point until he found soft stone.

"*Okoshikshak* we call it," Kayak said. "That means stone for making pots. It's good for carving." He held up a fist-sized piece of stone that he had broken off. "I asked this stone what's hiding inside. It won't answer me out loud, but I know there's a small owl hiding in there." He held it up. "Mattoosie, can you see it trying to get out?"

"Yes, I see it. That's its head," said Matt, "and that could be one wing."

"You're right," Kayak replied. Later, he laid his carving knife and file and flint and steel wool out before him. Thoughtfully he began his work.

Matthew took out of his packsack the only book he had brought with him. It was one his father had given him, called *Geology Made Easy*.

That evening Matthew said, "Your carving is starting to look just like an owl." He examined another smaller chunk of stone Kayak had brought back. "I believe this stone is called steatite or serpentine. It's a basalt, fairly soft and sometimes green with stripes. That's how it gets the name serpentine—because it looks like a serpent's skin.

"It says in this book that the kind of stone you're carving is most often found where there are deposits of silver and nickel," Matthew added.

"I didn't know that," Kayak said. "When I'm finished this carving, will you let me read that book?"

"Sure," said Matthew, "if you'll teach me to carve." He took up a third chunk of stone. "I see a bear crouching in this piece. It's a cub, I think, a small one that wouldn't hurt anyone. Maybe you'll lend me your carving knife and file and I'll see if I can let him out."

Two days later, they set their polished pair of carvings side by side.

"Your owl is a lot better than my bear," said Matthew.

"*Opinani!* No wonder!" Kayak answered. "My father's been teaching me to carve for two whole years. You make some more figures and they'll get better every time you carve one."

In the next few days they finished gathering and piling stones to mark more clearly the four seepage pools so that they could be found no matter how hard it snowed. After that they walked beyond their markers until they came to the large lake with a small waterfall that flowed down a short river feeding into the sea. The big lake was partly frozen over.

"When the tide rises," Kayak said, salt water floods into this lake."

As they watched, a large, red-bellied Arctic char rose at the edge of the ice and rolled, showing fin and tail.

"That's a big fish," Kayak said in excitement.

"Has this lake a name?" asked Matthew.

"None that I know," said Kayak. "I'll call the lake *Ikhalujuak*, after this. You can call it Big Fish Lake."

"If you are going to name this lake, I'm going to call that small island out there Black Skull Rock."

"I think we should move up here and make a winter camp," said Kayak. "We can set up the tents near that low cliff where there will be more protection from the wind. We've got to start to fish for food."

In the afternoon, the whole sky and the sea beyond the island's shores reflected the orange and yellow of the setting sun.

"Heavy winter's coming to us," Kayak said. "It's starting to get dark early and dawn is slow in coming. In December the sun won't rise at all."

That night under a full-faced moon they boiled the last two ptarmigan. Matt urged that they eat only one, even though their hunger was not satisfied.

It took three trips to carry their packsacks and supplies to their new campsite. Matt and Kayak stopped only once. That was when they heard the first wolf howl. It was answered by another somewhere along the edge of Big Fish Lake. Far out across the fog-bound, freezing sea they could hear a gasping, strangling sound.

"I don't mind the howling of the wolves," said Kayak. "They do that when the moon is getting full. It's that other ghostly sound out there that worries me."

"It seems to be coming from Black Skull Rock." Matthew shuddered and when Kayak looked at him, he pulled his hands inside his parka sleeves. "I'm not afraid. It's only that the weather's getting awfully cold."

"I'm not cold," said Kayak quietly, "but that sound does make me shiver."

X

RED EYES

IN THE MORNING, THERE WERE FROST CRYSTALS HANG-
ing like Christmas decorations on the inside walls
of their tent. Kayak crawled outside, then stuck his
head inside the tent again.

"The whole of Big Fish Lake has frozen over. By
tonight it may be strong enough to walk across. But,"
he added, "we're not going to try it—yet."

On the third day, they did go out. Kayak, using
the thick-bladed sheath knife that he had tied to the
short tent pole, tested the ice in advance of every
step they took.

"Mattoosie, you be careful. Only step exactly where
I step," Kayak called back to him. "I'm glad this lake
is tidal so the ice will bend. Sea ice bends a little
when you put your weight on it, because of the salt.

This lake ice is kind of half and half. Fresh-water ice is very dangerous. It breaks quick as glass and can drop you through without any warning."

"I got to start to chip open some fishing holes before this ice gets too thick. I hope we catch fish tomorrow. If they don't come back for us, we'll have to find something else to eat."

Matthew didn't like the sound of that.

Inside their darkened tent that night, they shared the last cold ptarmigan while sitting in their sleeping bags to keep warm. Again they heard the strangling, gasping sound.

"I'm going to light this candle," Kayak said. "It will make the tent seem nice and warm."

A wolf sent up its lonely howling. It was answered by another closer by.

"Oh, I wish my dad would get back here," said Matthew. "I'm getting *really* worried about them." He looked at the marks on the tent pole. "They've been gone for twenty-one days. I wonder," he said and bit his lip as he looked at Kayak, "I wonder if they could be lost again?"

Kayak looked up at the red tent's peak and did not answer, for he had been fearing that same thing for many days.

They lay in their sleeping bags and listened, hoping that somehow magically they would hear the distant throbbing of Matilda's whirling blades. Just outside the tent a frightening, crunching sound could be heard, something padding heavily toward them, breaking through the crust of snow as it came. Far out to sea they could hear the ghostly, strangling sound.

Matthew sat up in his sleeping bag and laid his hand upon the rifle. "Now we can hear something walking outside and the gurgling, dying sound. This place is getting as noisy as a city."

Kayak laughed at that, and so they pulled their sleeping bags over their heads and went to sleep.

Next morning, Kayak stuck his head outside their tent and shouted, "Fishing fills your belly and makes your troubles light." He was right.

They went out and knelt down at the fish holes, carefully lowering the hooks and lines that Charlie had left them for emergencies. By noon they had six fat, red-bellied Arctic char weighing about five pounds each.

"Don't throw away any heads or tails," said Kayak. "With whole fish you can make a lovely soup. This first one," he said, "I am going to cut it up and eat it just the way it is."

Matt didn't like the idea but he ate the fresh, raw fish with Kayak and discovered that it was delicious.

That evening, Kayak held the tent flap open. "Kicking kangaroos!" he said, in a voice that mimicked Charlie's.

When Matthew looked out, it was as though the sea around Black Skull Rock had been drained away, drunk up by some huge unseen elephant. The small island was white with autumn snow, but between them and it stretched a black, rock-strewn shore reaching out for a mile or more to where the water had receded.

"I never saw a big moon tide as low as that," said Kayak.

"And look over there," Matthew said. "It's as though a path connects this big island to Black Skull Rock. We could walk over there along the tidal flat. Tomorrow morning let's go and see what's causing all that moaning."

At dawn Kayak was up and pulling on his parka. "I wish we knew how long that tide's been out so we would know when it was coming in again."

"Hurry!" said Matthew. "We can walk fast, and the tide moves very, very slowly. Hurry up! Let's get started!"

Kayak pulled on his last pair of sealskin boots. "These are beginning to wear out, and when they do I'll be barefoot in the snow," he said to Matt.

Together they trotted to the shore and started out across the long tidal flats, avoiding the boulder-strewn areas, walking fast over the fine gravel or splashing through the shadow tide pools. It was a cold, windless morning with thin silver ice sheets clinging to the rocks. The fast walking kept them warm.

Kayak stopped and said, "We should have brought the rifle. Yuk! That's what's wrong with leaving camp in an awful hurry. We forgot the most important thing."

"No we didn't. I've got my geologist's hammer."

Matt showed Kayak that he had it stuck down through his belt. "Come on," Matthew said, starting to run. "That Black Skull Rock is not far now. We can be back at camp by noon."

The skull-shaped rock was much larger and farther away than Matthew had first judged. It was almost noon when the two boys finally climbed onto the huge smooth stone island.

They walked carefully over its whole tide-slick surface but could find no reason for the strange, heavy sounds that they had heard coming from it.

"I can't understand it," Kayak said. Then he grabbed Matthew by the arm and pointed to a dark mysterious cavern. "There it is," he whispered.

They examined its entrance cautiously. It was just big enough for them to bend and enter.

"Whatever causes that heavy breathing sound must live in there," said Matthew. "You go in and see."

"No, thank you, Mattoosie. You can go in first," said Kayak, "while I kick myself for coming here without the rifle."

"Why didn't we think to bring a flashlight?" Matthew whispered.

Curiosity overcame his fright and he ducked down and stepped through the rough stone entrance. Kayak forced himself to follow Matthew into the dark and dangerous-looking cave.

Inside the cave, Matthew was surprised to find that he could easily stand upright. He sniffed for gas, then struck a match.

"Why are you waiting there in the entrance?" he called to Kayak. "You'll never believe what you're going to see in here."

"Do you hear a giant gurgling sound?" Kayak asked him.

"No," said Matthew.

"That's good," said Kayak, and he came all the way inside.

Matthew struck a second match. As it flared up, they peered into the gloom and saw huge red eyes reflected in the match light.

Matt stepped close to Kayak and asked, "What are those?"

"There's another over there, and three more deep inside the cave."

"At first I thought those eyes were alive," said Matthew.

"What are they?" Kayak asked in a low voice.

Matthew stepped forward, reached up and carefully drew his fingers across the nearest pair that were embedded in the wall. "They're cold and sharp," said Matthew. "I think they may be garnets. Big ones!"

He took the sharp end of his rock hammer and tapped the stone beside the gem. Three times he struck it, and on the fourth blow a huge almost perfect garnet fell loose into his hand.

"I've never before seen a red one as big or clear as this," he said in wonder. "Not even in the museums in Mexico or Arizona."

"Ariz-ooona!" Kayak said and laughed. "Mattoosie,

you must love Arizooona. Everything that's good or big comes from Arizooona, you tell me, or Peru. Are those stones worth more than gold?"

"Oh, no," Matthew said. "But some people are always looking for perfect big red gems like this."

He went and tapped another. It fell out easily.

"Holy cow," he gasped. "I'm going to fill my pockets and my parka hood with these."

"Me, too," said Kayak. "I'm starting to like these shiny stones."

They paused and gobbled down their bully beef and hardtack biscuits, then took turns with the geologist's hammer. Using its sharp steel claw, they loosened the huge, red, winking garnets from the worn walls of the cave. Eager to take as many as they could, they lost all sense of time.

"Mattoosie, what's that sound?" asked Kayak.

Matthew was so busy loosening a beautiful egg-sized garnet that he scarcely heard the sound at first.

Huuh-uuh. Auuh-uuuuh!

"It's the heavy strangling sound." Matthew gasped in fear, as he peered into the shadowy blackness of the cave. "It's come back again."

Together they stood listening in horror.

Huuh-uuh. Auuh-uuuuh! The strange, sad, frightening sighing came to them again, followed by a low gurgling sound like some captured giant choking, drowning deep inside the rocky cave.

"Quick, run out of here," Kayak urged. "I think I

know what's making that sound. I'm dead afraid of this place!"

"What's causing it?" Matthew asked. "It sounds like . . . it is! It's water!"

Even as he spoke, sea water came flooding over the whole floor of the cave.

"Get out! Get out!" Kayak yelled. "The tide is rising. We can't get caught in here. We'll drown!"

Matthew bent and ran splashing after Kayak. Once outside they were shocked to see that the water had flooded in all around Black Skull Rock.

"If we run along that high gravel ridge, I think we might still make it back to the main island," Kayak said.

Together they started running. But the loose wet gravel slowed their stride. The long black highway that curved toward their camp on Prince Charles Island was already disappearing in the tide. They splashed forward until the water reached their boot tops.

"It's going to be too deep," said Kayak, when the water reached his thighs. "We'll have to turn back and wait until tomorrow when the tide goes out again."

"Tomorrow?" Matthew gasped, as they looked back in terror at Black Skull Rock. "You mean we've got to stay out here all night long?"

Kayak stared up at the sky. "There's no wind and no sign of bad weather," he said. "We might be lucky.

Even the smallest storm would wash us off this rock and drown us in the night."

"I hate the thought of staying here," said Matthew, as they climbed back onto the dead black rock.

"Tonight the moon is sure to draw one of the biggest tides to come in all the year. But if we're still alive, we should be able to leave early in the morning." Kayak's teeth were chattering and his face looked blue. "Take off your boots and socks and put your bare feet under my parka. I'll wring your socks out. Then you put them on again with your boots. Then you do the same for me and we'll trot around the rock until our feet warm up."

When that was done, they squatted on Black Skull Rock, waiting, watching in fear as the huge tide edged in around them. In the moonlight, their small tent on Prince Charles Island seemed a million miles away. They watched the deadly waters rise and could think of nothing else. Heavy storm clouds gathered across the moon.

"I can't hear or see it rising any more," said Kayak with a sigh of relief, for the freezing waters were almost at their feet.

They curled up in the darkness and sucked in their stomachs to ease their hunger as they tried to fall asleep and forget the towering gray banks of icy fog that stood all around them in the cold and fearsome night that had swallowed up the moon.

Just before dawn, Matthew shivered and jerked

wide awake. He shook Kayak, saying, "What's that smell? It smells to me like pigs."

Kayak woke and sniffed the air. "*Ivik! Ivik!* he whispered. "Walrus. You smell walrus. Oh, that's very bad! Listen and you'll hear them. I'm afraid they're coming up. They're climbing up behind us onto this rock."

Now Matthew could not only smell the walrus, he could hear them as they moved through the water making low grunting sounds.

"We've picked the worst place in the world," moaned Kayak, as he crouched and stared out at the cold gray tide waters that stretched all around them. "We're on a walrus rock. I can tell by the sounds they're making," he told Matthew, "that there are a great many of them."

Kayak climbed up and peered over the curved stone crest of Black Skull Rock, then slid back down beside Matthew.

"It's much worse than I thought," he said. "I'm sorry to tell you, Mattoosie, I don't think we are going to get back to our big island alive."

"Why do you say that?" Matthew asked, as he felt cold fear rise in him.

"You go up there and look," said Kayak. "You'll see."

Matthew crawled to the rock crest and peered over. He counted three, four, five, six, seven massive bull walrus. Each had huge curved ivory tusks. White bristles thrust out from their upper lips. These enormous animals had pulled themselves out of the water onto the edge of the smooth black rocks. Around each one of them Matthew could see a close-packed herd of female walrus, sleeker than the males, with thin polished tusks. The females were pulling themselves out of the water using their powerful front and rear flippers, crowding close to the particular bull walrus that jealously protected them.

"There are hundreds of them," Matthew gasped. "Bigger than hippopotamuses! They must be dangerous."

"Don't let any of those walrus near you," Kayak warned him, especially those big bulls. My father says when they are guarding their females, they are afraid of nothing. They will even attack a huge iron ship!"

Matthew watched in horror as more and more enormous walrus heaved up onto Black Skull Rock. The deep-throated bellowing noise of the herd increased. He had to shout to Kayak to make himself heard above the savage grunting of the animals.

Countless dark heads bobbed in the water, flashing their bright ivory tusks, their breaths steaming white in the freezing morning air as they tried to crowd onto the rock.

"There will never be enough space here for all," said Kayak. "But every one of them will try to rest here. They must be tired from swimming. They've probably been stuffing their bellies full of clams. Now all they want to do is crowd together on this island and sleep."

"When will the tide go down enough for us to get away from here?" asked Matthew in a shaky voice.

"That's the trouble, Mattoosie. It's not going to go out soon enough to save us from them."

One huge bull appeared on the very crest of the island, and then another. Ignoring the two boys, they bellowed out a fighting challenge to each other. Females appeared around them and then like lava that comes flowing out of a volcano, they humped their huge chocolate brown bulks over the rise and came pouring down toward the first humans they had ever seen. The two bull walrus roared in rage, warning each other away from their females. Kayak took Matthew by the arm and together they retreated down from the low crest of the island toward the water's edge.

Now, before them and on both sides of them in the icy black waters they could see countless walrus pushing toward them on the slippery rock.

"Shake hands and say good-by to me, Mattoosie. We have only got a few more minutes before we get pushed into the water. So I say good-by, my brother."

Matthew stared at Kayak in utter desperation. The enormous herd thrust all around them until their eyes and ears and noses were filled with the frightful vision, the deafening roar and the overwhelming smell.

Kayak did the only thing left for them to do. He

grabbed Matthew by the arm and stepped carefully knee-deep onto the slippery rock beneath the water. Matthew followed him. They could hear the heavy slap of flippers as walrus pressed behind them. The tide was going out and the long gravel neck that stretched to the main island could now be partly seen.

Turning their backs to the water, Kayak and Matthew looked up in horror at the hellish sight of close-packed walrus surging toward them, totally covering Black Skull Rock.

One of the younger bull walrus slipped on the seaweed and slithered dangerously close to a huge old bull. Quick to defend his females, the old walrus reared back and drove his thick curved tusks into the bulging neck muscles of the younger male. Behind them, the females in the big bulls' herds stopped swaying and were silent, sensing that they were about to witness a fearful battle. The younger bull, whose white ivory tusks had been sharpened by constant digging in the clam beds, let out a roar of pain and anger as it lunged at the heavier walrus, ripping two long gashes in its tough leather hide. The fight was on!

Matthew and Kayak took another fearful step out into the water on the island's edge as the two sea beasts fought their deadly battle less than a dozen paces from them. But even as they watched, the boys realized that these two fighting animals were the only reason that the large herd of female walrus did not come surging forward, forcing them to their deaths in the freezing water.

The violence of the struggle between the two bull walrus, the roaring, the thrust of tusks, the slashing blows made Matthew forget his fear and watch in wonder.

As the two bulls tired of the fight, their mighty muscles trembled beneath their scarred and bleeding sides and their attacks became weaker and fewer. Their breath pumped out like steam into the frosty air. The females remained in separate herds just behind the fighting bulls, watching intently, ready to leave the loser and go over to the winner's side.

Matthew jumped when Kayak touched his arm.

"It's over. We got to try to get away," Kayak said. "Be very careful not to slip. When they see us move, they'll get excited. Quick! Let's run for it!"

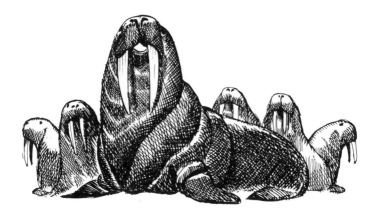

XI

DISCOVERY NUMBER THREE

"YOU CAN SEE IT NOW," YELLED KAYAK. "THE RIDGE over to the big island is rising as the tide flows out."

Supporting each other, they stepped cautiously away from the slippery edge of the walrus rock and struggled waist-deep through the freezing sea. They were in deep water only for a few minutes. Soon Matthew could feel the loose gravel beneath his feet sloping upward, and before he knew it they were knee deep, then only ankle deep in water. As the big moon tide ran out, they crossed the rising gravel ridge. They were running free!

Matthew turned and looked back at Black Skull Island. The whole smooth rock was now entirely covered with walrus whose great brown bodies packed together looked like tide-worn boulders. The walrus herd lay resting there silently as they had each early winter for countless centuries before the coming of man.

"We're lucky," Kayak gasped. "I thought we'd never leave that rock alive."

A sharp wind was rising and they could feel a thin sheath of ice forming on their soaking boots and trousers.

"Let's go. I'm freezing cold," said Matthew.

"We'll run back to the tent," said Kayak. "Running will keep us warm."

And so it did.

Inside the tent, they lit the small primus stove and put on a full kettle of water to boil. They hung up their wet clothing and jumped into their sleeping bags. From there they shared the last tin of dried beef and a hardtack biscuit while they heated one of their last packages of dried beef soup.

"I hope I dream of Arizona or Peru or some warm sunny place like that," said Matthew as he wriggled down inside his bag.

"If you do," said Kayak, "be sure to take me with you in your dream, because I wish to see that country —Arizoooona. I want to know how the Apache hunters signal with their mirrors. I want to see anti-loops running, and that tall yellow food that grows out of the ground. Mattoosie, you remember I've never seen a cow or horse or tree except in pictures."

Before Matthew could answer him they both fell asleep. But Matthew did not dream of Arizona, and in the morning he was still dreaming of an enormous hungry polar bear, which was not at all the dream that he had chosen.

Suddenly Kayak shook him by the arm and shouted, "Mattoosie! Can you hear it? Listen!"

Off to the southeast, Matthew could hear a faint *chop-chop-chop-chop-chop* that was growing louder, louder, louder.

"It's them. It must be Matilda!" Matthew yelled and leaped out of his sleeping bag, unzipped the tent and stood outside. "There she is!" He pointed at Matilda's bright red hull zooming through the cold blue morning sky. Clad only in his boots and long white winter underwear, he waved his arms and did a joyful dance.

"Get dressed, Mattoosie. Get some pants on and your parka," Kayak shouted. He, too, waved up at Matilda as she passed like trembling thunder just above their heads.

"Holy smoke," said Matthew, sounding like his father. "It's going to be all right! They *didn't* get lost!"

Matilda landed not more than twenty paces from their tent. Matt's father slid back the helicopter's door and ducked out to greet them. "You two look like you're still alive and hearty," he shouted. Then he grabbed them both in a big bear hug. "I've been worried about you every day we've been away."

"We were worried about you, too," said Matthew.

"It is good to see you back," said Kayak. "We got

something to tell you later—about what we found out on that skull-shaped island."

"Are you starving?" Charlie asked them. "You must have used up all your food at least a week ago."

"We caught some fish and ptarmigan. We didn't starve," said Matt.

"That's fine!" said Matthew's father. "But still I guess you could use some orange juice and a pan of nice fresh eggs for breakfast?"

"Fresh eggs?" whispered Kayak.

"Orange juice?" Matthew gasped. "We've forgotten what things like that look like. You serve them up, and we'll tell you how they taste."

"Fresh food's not the only thing we flew in here with us," said Charlie. "We've brought along a truly famous chef. *Ta-taa!*" he sang and waved like a master of ceremonies toward Matilda.

Dr. Wolfgang Volks smiled as he stepped through Matilda's door.

He took off his thick-lensed glasses and wiped the steam away. "So"—he spread his arms in greetings—"I meet you two boys at last. Charlie and your father have been speaking every day about you. I promise you, they're mighty glad to see you both standing safe beside your little tent. And me, too, I'm glad to see you! *Das ist wünderbar!*" He snatched off one huge mitt and shook hands with both of them.

Professor Volks was not more than five feet four inches tall and wore a furry, Russian-looking winter hat. He was dressed in a thick blue quilted jumpsuit that covered him from head to foot. Even through the professor's glasses Kayak could see that the old man's gray-blue eyes had a quick and lively twinkle in them as though everything in the whole world interested him intensely. His cheeks were red, which made his whole face cheerful.

"I'll be the cook," said Dr. Volks. "I want to observe the changes in the eggs we brought for you. I'm studying the effects of extreme temperatures on soft materials. Excuse me," he said. "I'll cook these eggs before they freeze." He paused as he headed for the tent and looked around him at the bleak white landscape. "Tell me, boys, why did you have to discover oil in such a faraway place?" He stamped his fleece-lined Arctic boots and flapped his arms to drive away the cold. "You might have found it somewhere south of here. Maybe St. Petersburg in Florida or on one of those beautiful Hawaiian islands would have been a better place to strike the oil."

"Oh, you're going to really like it in my country!" Kayak said. "I was born not so far from here. I can tell you it's a lovely place to live! You ask Mattoosie. We've had good times and peaceful weather—ever since that one bad blizzard blew away from here."

In no time at all the professor had helped them rearrange the tents. He sang happily as he prepared breakfast on their small primus stove. Even with the flap partly open, it filled the tent with welcome warmth.

"I never smelled anything better than that in my whole life," said Kayak, as he sniffed the cooking eggs and bacon and heard the grease crackling in the pan.

"You're right," said Matthew. He held a chunk of bread with Charlie's pliers and tried to toast it on the edge of the flame.

Only when the cooking heat rose all around him did the professor finally take off his long-flapped Russian hat. Kayak noticed that he had a fringe of wispy silver hair around his large bald head. His hands were delicate and all his movements were quick and precise, as he neatly laid out everything with care. He put knives here, forks there, salt and pepper lined up exactly with their mugs of coffee.

"*Achtung!*" he said, and Kayak and Matt held out their tin plates. The professor gave them each three strips of bacon and three eggs, then quickly broke a dozen more into the pan.

"Sir, I'm glad you're a good cook," said Matthew. "We've been eating nothing much for weeks but fish and ptarmigan. It's wonderful to have bacon and eggs again."

When they had eaten all that they could hold, Matt's father said, "There, I'll bet that feels better."

"We've got a big lightweight tent packed inside Matilda, as well as a powerful radio transceiver good for both sending and receiving. I tell you boys"—Charlie laughed—"we got some grand surprises for you in that helicopter. Just you wait and see. Kayak, your grandmother sent you and Matt each two new pairs of sealskin boots."

Heavy snow began to fall and it took them most of the rest of the day to rebuild their base camp. They arranged the three tents in a neat triangle, just right for winter living, with a narrow snow trail leading from one entrance to another. The new tent was much larger inside than the two sleeping tents. It was designed in a round form like an igloo to stand up against the foulest weather.

"It's a general tent for all of us, though Dr. Volks will sleep here," Matt's father told them. "We will keep most of our equipment in this general tent: supplies, the radio, instruments and maps. We'll all meet in here together and use this long folding table for eating, and for making plans as well." He arranged the pressure lamp above it. "We'll still use the two smaller tents for sleeping."

The camp stood near enough to the lake so they could draw fresh water through the ice while the low stone cliff near their stone marker number two protected them from the violence of the north wind.

Early the next morning, the sky was clear. Mr. Morgan stood outside the boys' sleeping tent and shouted, "Matt! Kayak! Is this our lucky day? Is this the day that brings us our black diamonds?"

At the very mention of those magic words, Charlie unzipped their tent flap and hollered in to them, "Get ready laddos, today's the day to make our fortunes!"

Matt and Kayak crawled out of their sleeping bags and hurried into their pants and new sealskin boots and parkas. They saw Dr. Volks step outside the larger nylon tent. He shivered, pulled up the wide cuffs on his heavy outer mitts, and pulled down the long ear flaps on his furry hat. There was no wind, but it was so cold it made the snow squeal underneath their feet.

"Those two stone markers," said Charlie, "are the main sites where Matt and Kayak discovered the oil seepage. The other two are over that hill."

The professor peered at the two gray rock markers nearest them. He shouted, "*Wünderbar!* Looks to me like upper paleozoic with, I hope, strong subsalt and mesozoic plays. Lead me to the other two sites, please. We must investigate."

"Mattoosie, is Dooctoor Voooks talking in some different language?" Kayak whispered.

"No," Matt answered, "but don't you worry. I can't really understand what he's saying either."

Dr. Volks felt through the depths of his deep Arctic pockets. Finally, he managed to haul out of his down-filled costume a large pocket watch. It was attached to him somewhere by a long, strong silver chain.

"Seven forty-two A.M. plus thirty-one seconds," the professor stated. "Let us go and begin our work. Tell me, boys, which site do you choose first? We can eat our breakfast there."

Kayak and Matt whispered together then pointed

to the marker at the base of the cliff, the one they called Number Three.

"That one there," said Kayak. "Mattoosie and me, we both think three's our lucky number."

"Boys, please go to the big tent and bring me twelve fresh eggs, and the frying pan, and a nice fat pat of butter," said the professor.

When Matthew and Kayak returned, the well-wrapped butter went into Dr. Volks' pocket. Then he took off his fur-lined hat, placed the eggs inside, and very carefully put it on his head again. Matthew began to giggle when he saw that.

"Well," said Dr. Volks, "where else would you carry twelve fresh eggs this morning, if you wanted to keep them warm, not freezing?"

"I don't know," said Matthew, truthfully.

"Where would you put them?" the professor asked Kayak.

"I'd carry them just where you've got them," said Kayak. "Inuit never get eggs in the winter, but in spring when it's warmer, we let down our parka hoods and carry them in there."

"Did you hear that?" said Dr. Volks thumping on the frying pan as though it were a drum. "You two boys and Charlie bring the shovels. We will do a little digging."

He started to march off, following Matt's father, who was already striding out toward marker Number Three. "Just a minute," the professor called. "We have to bring our little camp stove. There's no driftwood on this island. How are we going to cook?"

As Kayak ran back to get the cooking stove, Charlie whispered in Matt's ear, "I know of another way to fry an egg out there."

When they were gathered around Number Three discovery well, the professor knelt down and carefully examined the windblown rocks. He said, "Such a strong overlay of marine shale could indicate high gravity oil with good porosity." The long flaps on his fur hat dangled in the Arctic breeze as Dr. Volks sniffed along the stone crack of Number Three discovery site.

"*Wünderbar!*" He chuckled. "Gentlemen, I think you really have found it! I just got a strong sniff of natural gas. It smells like this sedimentary basin could be filled up to the spill point."

"Let's eat some breakfast before we get to our serious work," said Charlie.

"Why don't you go far over there behind those rocks against the cliff," Dr. Volks suggested, "then light that little stove you brought with you." The professor carefully removed his hat and gave Charlie all the eggs.

"Maybe we don't need a little stove to do our cooking," Charlie remarked, as he slipped a book of matches from his pocket. He bent down over the long gray crack in the rock, sniffed, then struck a match.

"What are you doing?" screamed Professor Volks. "Are you trying to kill us all?"

He crouched in horror and clapped his hands over

his ears to protect himself from the terrible explosion.

The match that Charlie struck had failed to light.

Hearing nothing, Dr. Volks opened his eyes and shouted, "Charlie! You gave me such an awful fright. Lighting matches around here is the most dangerous thing that anyone could do.

"You do the cooking this morning, but please, go far away from here unless you want to see us all go flying through the air!"

"I'll be careful with the matches," Charlie promised, "if you will tell us, professor—what do we do after breakfast?"

The professor smiled as he polished his steamy glasses. "First we have to run field tests on all four seepage points."

XII

CALLING FIRELAND

THAT NIGHT DR. VOLKS SPENT HUNCHED OVER THE TABLE
in the main tent, working with his small computer
calculator, spirit level, and a special slide rule. He
made hundreds of complicated calculations and equa-
tions on dozens of sheets of yellow paper while the
pressure lantern burned and the air grew murky in
the tent.

In the morning, Matthew's father said, "What do
your think, Professor Volks?"

"I believe," said the professor, "that we have millions and millions of barrels of oil and trillions of
cubic feet of natural gas lying in a mammoth natural
storage vault underneath our feet." He pointed down.
"I cannot tell yet how big the seismic field will be, or
exactly how deep it goes, or guess precisely the cubic

feet of gas it might contain. I'm just jumping to find out about that sedimentary basin.

Mr. Morgan shouted, "Charlie, is there a mug of coffee you can spare?"

"I've been working for years and years," said the professor, "perfecting some very light drilling equipment. It's said to be the smallest in the world. I designed it so that it can easily be shipped to here or there or . . . anywhere. And this place," he said, "is certainly . . . anywhere. Even a small company can test drill the net-pay thickness of a find. The whole drill rig will pack into a large C-119 type aircraft."

"Whoowh!" said Charlie. "Can you get all the drilling equipment we would need into a single aircraft?"

"I designed it for that purpose," said Professor Volks.

"Where is this equipment now?" Matt's father asked.

"It's on the east slope of the mountains in a place called Fireland, Patagonia, at the southern tip of South America. That's a wild and wonderful country. They say Magellan, the early explorer, feared to land his ship there because it looked like hell to him with the mountains spouting fire. That drill rig of mine has just touched the lower Jurassic sandstone on a number of deep drillings, but so far, not a drop of oil."

"Could we ever manage to get your light rig up onto this island?" Matthew's father asked him.

The professor rubbed his nose to warm it up. "We'll never know unless we try. Maybe if I ask them, that company will help us out, I mean lend us the right airplane and my equipment. But could we find a place here to land such a huge flying box car?"

"That frozen lake out there," said Charlie, "is almost like a long, flat landing strip. It would be the best place to land a 119 aircraft . . . but only when the ice is thick."

Dr. Volks turned to Matt's father. "If you wish, I'll tell the company that we have a good chance here for an important oil and gas strike."

"That's fine," Ross Morgan said. "What name are you boys going to call this new company?"

"How about the Kayak-Matthew Company?" said Charlie. "Those two lads found it and it should bear their names."

"Too plain," said Matthew. "We want to call it the Kayamatt Drilling Company."

Kayak and Matthew laughed and shook hands together.

"Imagine us being brothers and partners in a company," Kayak said.

The professor waited until darkness came, when radio short wave signals would be at their very best. He carefully adjusted the large knob and began tuning with the small dial of the transceiver. At 8:00 P.M. it crackled into life.

"XK2 YUW Northwest Territories, Canada, XK2

YUW calling Radio PQR3, *Fireland,* calling PQR3 *Fireland,* Patagonia, Argentina. Calling Radio Fireland, Do you read me? *Atención! Atención!* Over."

The answer came back. "*Aquí Radio PQR3 Fireland. Lo oimos con toda claridad, Profesor. Hable, por favor. Cambio.*"

Their radio transceiver coughed up a dozen high speed codes and languages from all around the world as the professor tuned the dials finely and blew into the microphone. Then he spoke in rapid Spanish.

As he listened to the answer, his glasses steamed up. He spoke again. He tapped the microphone for luck and winked an eye at Matt and Kayak.

"*Wünderbar!* It's just as I had hoped. They say they will pack up my new drill rig *mui pronto* and shoehorn all of it into their C-119 aircraft and fly it up here. The manager is sending for their pilot to speak with us. They say he has never flown in the Arctic although he's ferried supplies to the South Pole in the Antarctic and understands whiteout conditions and most other problems of cold weather flying. You have a word with him, Charlie. They say their pilot speaks good English."

"Baffinland to Patagonia . . . hello there, chummy!" Charlie called into the microphone as if he'd known the other pilot all his life. "I suggest you load up that 119 of yours and fly it to Rio, then north to Montreal. Fuel up, then fly to Goose Bay on the Labrador coast, then to Frobisher on southeast Baffin Island. You can find those places on your map quicker than I can say duck-billed platypus. After that the whole thing gets very tricky."

Charlie tapped the microphone. "You still there, chummy? I've got a Mounted Police pilot friend of mine named Sergeant Fletcher. You can pick him up in Frobisher. He's a first rate Arctic flyer. I'll send him a coded message and tell him where to find us. You'll have to land here on the ice. We'll lay out a strip on the ice long enough to take a C-119. The ice is getting thicker every day. It should soon support your weight."

"You make damn sure of that!" the Patagonian pilot shouted through his microphone. "I only like hot baths. I . . ."

Gobby . . . wobby . . . luk . . .

"Signals are going down," Charlie shouted. "Talk to you tomorrow, chummy. Over and out."

"That's a lovely little radio you've got there," said Charlie, admiring all its dials and switches. "I wish I had one as strong as that inside Matilda."

"You will, you will," said the professor. "If you're not careful, you'll be a millionaire before you know it, Charlie. Are you ready to be rich?" he asked.

"You bet your ruddy boots I am." Charlie chuckled. "I'll go lie under a breadfruit tree in Tahiti and study island dancing."

"You don't look like a lazy man to me," said Dr. Volks.

In the next two weeks they all had to practice being lazy. Charlie didn't even move Matilda. The weather grew colder. They heard no further word from Patagonia. All they could do was wait, wait, wait and hope that the ice would thicken.

At twelve noon on the nineteenth day, it was clear and bright. "Boys, would you like to see a miracle?" the professor said. "It's an experiment I've been wanting to make, but I had to hold off until the weather was perfect." He held out his hand like a magician and showed them something blue.

"What is that?" asked Matthew.

"It's an ordinary measuring spoon that women use in the kitchen," said Professor Volks. "I chose it because it's made of smooth plastic and it's perfectly round in shape, not too shallow, not too deep." He filled it slowly with water from their kettle.

"What are you going to do with it?" Kayak asked.

"Follow me and you will see." The professor stepped outside the tent and said, "Just right! Bright sunshine and very, very cold." He carefully set the round spoon in the snow. "At this temperature it should only take a few minutes. Kayak, you count to one hundred in Eskimo and in English."

Kayak began. "One—*atouasik*. Two—*muko*. Three —*pingashut* . . ."

When he stopped, the professor said, "A lovely sounding language. I'd like to try and learn to speak *Inuktitut*. But first we must check our round spoon to see there are no bubbles."

"It's frozen solid," Kayak said.

"Our experiment continues," the professor added,

and drew a piece of toilet tissue from his parka pocket. "Kayak, please be careful when you pop that piece of ice out of the spoon. Hold its edges. Don't mark its surface with your fingers. Look at the position of the sun. You can try to focus the sun's image through the ice lens as though it were a magnifying glass." He handed Kayak the soft white paper. "Focus the bright spot of light on this," he said. "Make the sun's spot very, very small."

Before Kayak could count ten the bright dot on the tissue turned brown, then black, began to smoke, then burst into flame.

"*Voilà!*" said the professor. "Fire through ice!"

"*Wakudlunga!*" Kayak gasped in disbelief. "That is truly frozen fire. I never saw anything like that before. My grandfather would have said that proves this world is full of magic."

"Your grandfather would have been right," the professor said. "The more I think about this world the more I know that it is magical. Every day when the sun rises, it is to me a miracle!"

That night, Charlie opened the tent flap and said, "Step out here and see another miracle—right above our heads."

Matt looked up and saw the northern lights moving like dozens of enormous searchlights probing through the stars.

Kayak raised his arms and whistled at the lights. They seemed to come and go as though they followed his hand movements. "My grandfather says those are giants up there playing kickball with a skull. Could that be true?"

"Why not?" said the professor. "We don't know exactly what causes the aurora borealis, or as you say, northern lights. Maybe, just maybe, your grandfather could be right. I can bet you one thing," the professor said, "our radio will have lots of static and we won't hear much while that kicking game up there is going on."

He was right. For the next ten days on the radio they heard only noisy jumble.

Each noon they measured and every day the ice grew thicker.

Five mornings later, it was truly cold. The professor crawled out of his sleeping bag and said, "I wonder how thick that ice is now?"

"We could measure our fishing holes and let you know," said Kayak.

The professor handed each of them a long steel rule. "Measure the ice depth very carefully, boys, and come straight back."

"You measure the first hole in inches," Matthew said, "and I'll measure the second in centimeters. That way we will do a double-check."

They crossed the ice quickly. "Thirty-six inches and a little bit. *Avitilo-kolitlo-pingasho-aktuklo-kit-apilo*," Kayak said. "That's the way Inuit say it."

At the second hole Matthew measured. "Exactly ninety centimeters."

They hurried back across the lake through the

bitter early winter cold and when they reached the tent, Matthew said to the professor in Eskimo, "The ice is *avitilo-kolitlo-pingasho-aktuklo-kitapilo*."

"That's interesting," the professor said. "Does that mean thirty-six and a bit?"

"Yes," said Matthew.

"*Wakudlunga!*" Kayak gasped. "He understands *Inuktitut* already."

"Oh, no." The professor laughed. "But I learn a little. I like the sounds of languages and the way different kinds of peoples build them. Both German and English are rather confusing languages, though quite good for opera singers and for poets. And also I have to admit that William Shakespeare made very good use of his native tongue."

"The ice, professor," Charlie murmured. "Can you tell us about the safety of the *ice!*"

The professor adjusted his glasses and held up his hand as if he were in a classroom, "Yah, I will concentrate all my thoughts on the strength of thirty-six inches of ice, or ninety centimeters, and how it will support XYZ pounds, or XYZ kilos of weight, in this cold reading of minus 40 degrees Celsius or minus 40 degrees Fahrenheit. Strange that they should be the same; it's the only time that that occurs."

Together they stood at the end of the table and watched the professor swiftly jabbing his right forefinger at his computer, then with his left hand noting masses of figures on the yellow paper. For a long time he spoke to no one.

Finally he looked up at Matthew's father and said, "That makes a very, very difficult equation, but I feel sure the ice is just about thick enough. Tonight we can try calling Fireland radio to give them the go ahead."

"I heard Dr. Volks tapping away at his calculator this morning long before dawn," said Kayak quietly to Matthew.

"Yes," Matthew answered. "I guess he's worried."

"I would be, too, working in theoretical mathematics," said Matthew's father. "If calculations are wrong . . . wham! crack! slurp! The ice will break and the pilot, plane and everything in it may go down through the ice—forever."

"Don't talk like that," said Dr. Volks, who had stopped work and was listening. "You frighten me! Have you got a transit level?"

"I have," Matt's father nodded.

Professor Volks said, "The only way I now see it is to mark out the airstrip for them on the ice. When they come in to land, we watch the plane's wheels. If your transit level shows the ice level going down under their weight, then we all wave madly to their pilot, telling him to take off quick and fly away. What do you think?"

Charlie and Ross Morgan looked at each other.

Ross Morgan said, "I don't know any other method. I guess we'll have to try that."

"Let's go out and make an Arctic airstrip for them," Charlie said. "That's something I know how to do."

Charlie had them tear up a small red nylon tarpaulin into long narrow strips of cloth.

On their way out onto the ice, Charlie carefully studied the snowdrifts on the lake.

"The prevailing wind here is from the northwest. Is that right?" Charlie called to Kayak.

"Yes," Kayak answered, as he kicked the wind-packed drifts.

They tied the red strips around small snow blocks that they cut to hold the markers and laid out their long airstrip. It was almost half a mile in length and more than one hundred feet in width along the center of the snow-covered lake, heading straight northwest. Charlie set up a collapsible metal pole with a long red flag attached to show the pilot the wind direction.

"Just pray there's not an ice fog when they're coming in," said Charlie. "I'm still worried about the thickness of this salty ice. What if it won't hold them?"

"I don't know any other way to gauge it." Professor Volks sighed.

"Excuse me, Dooctoor Voooks," said Kayak. "I might know a way to tell."

"How is that?" the professor asked him.

"Well, I learned this from my grandfather," Kayak said in a shy, unsure voice. "He told me that, to test the strength of salt ice, make a small hole in it and press down your foot near the hole. If the ice is bending, it will force water up through the hole. You can easily see the water spouting even when you can't see the ice sagging. If the ice is very strong, it won't change and no water will come up."

"Remarkable!" said the professor. "That sounds simple and it sounds just right!" He clapped his mittened hands together. "Continue, Kayak. Tell us more."

"If we cut a few more small holes in this ice," said Kayak, "when that heavy plane lands, if water starts to shoot up through those holes, we will know that the weight of the plane is pressing down too hard. We'll all wave flags to warn the pilots to take off again without allowing the heavy plane to stop."

"Now, that's what I call native intelligence," the professor said. "Your grandfather," he said, "was a very smart man, Kayak. You come from observant people. I wish I always had such clever thoughts as that."

"Matthew," said his father. "Will you and Kayak take that homemade chisel of his and cut about six more small holes in the ice along the edge of Charlie's airstrip? Kayak will know just where to place them."

"I'm going down to the sea ice and check the grandfather's theory, though I'm quite sure it's going to work," said the professor.

"Sila, please get colder," Kayak called up to the sky. "We want that ice to get a little fatter belly underneath."

"Who's Sila?" asked Professor Volks.

"She's the spirit who controls the weather," Kayak answered.

That night the professor turned on his transceiver.

"XK2, YUW, XK2, YUW. Foxe Basin, Canada, calling Flight Control Frobisher. Do you read me? Do you read me? Over."

"*Oui, certainement, petite isle.*"

"*Bon!*" the professor answered. "*Est-ce que le C-119 est arrivé a Frobisher maintenant?*"

"*Pas encore. Nous avions eu une message de New York. Il arrivera ici demain matin.*"

The professor turned and smiled at Matt and Kayak. "They say our plane's due in Frobisher tomorrow."

Two days later, the weather was clear and their test holes had been chipped out. They advised Flight Control Frobisher that the big transport plane could now come in.

Just before noon on the following day, on the morning of November 19th, they heard the rumbling thunder of four engines as the heavy plane came soaring in from the southwest.

"Oh, that plane is big!" said Kayak.

The professor was hurrying along the snow-drifted ice toward the end of Charlie's makeshift runway. Even at that distance Matt could tell that he, like all of them, was bursting with excitement.

The huge aircraft circled once as the pilot examined the new airstrip, then it flew east, turned, and came in, wheels down. Matthew heard the pitch of the engines change. The big aircraft lowered its tail and wing flaps and raised its nose cap like a huge sea eagle coming in to land. It skimmed just above the hard-packed snow, cautiously preparing to ease its full weight onto the unknown strength of the rubbery salt ice.

"*Achtung! Achtung!* Watch the fish holes!" the professor shouted. He leaped about and waved his hands. He was shouting something but no one could hear him over the tremendous whining roar of the aircraft's giant, throbbing engines.

The wheels touched and Matt saw the first pair of holes spurt water into the air like twin jet fountains. As the airplane thundered down the icy runway, Matthew closed his eyes in horror.

XIII

ARCTIC WILD CAT

WHEN MATTHEW OPENED HIS EYES AGAIN, THE HUGE transport plane was running beside the fourth set of small fish holes. The water bubbled out over the ice but did not spurt into the air as it had with the first two. When the aircraft reached the sixth set of holes where Matt was waiting, the water came up not at all. He, like Kayak, the professor and his father, leaped in the air with joy.

The big plane slowed, then wheeled around in a tight circle and came trundling back toward them, its four big engines blowing a blizzard of fine snow into the air. When the plane stopped, Charlie raced out onto the runway toward the heavy transport that was already swinging open its enormous door.

"Get a wiggle on, Charlie boy," shouted his friend, Sergeant Fletcher, who had taken on the task of navigating the big plane. "Let's unload this tight-packed stuff." His breath blew out like steam.

"It's awful damn cold up here," said the Danish pilot, "and we got to get back to Frobisher tonight. Would any of you like a ride back there with us?"

"Not ruddy likely." Charlie laughed. "We're staying right here on this snowflake farm to make our fortunes." He shivered. "This blooming climate round here's lovely. I threw my toothbrush water out the tent this morning. It turned into one long sharp icicle before it hit the snow."

The pilot of the heavy transport plane jumped down onto the snow and said, "I'm from Copenhagen and believe me, we Danish never had to put up with weather like this."

"How about Greenland?" Charlie shouted. "You trying to tell me your fellow Greenlanders grow oranges and bananas way up there?"

"Dr. Volks," the Danish pilot shouted to him. "You want me to drive this little yellow monster of yours out of the belly hold?"

"That's no monster. That wonderful machine is Hansel. He is mighty wise and quick for only three years old. Don't touch him. I'll move little Hansel out myself," he said and heaved himself up, disappearing inside the huge metal belly of the airplane.

In a few minutes, Kayak and Matthew heard a

rumbling sound and down the loading ramp came the strangest looking vehicle that either of them had ever seen. It was painted bright yellow and shaped rather like an army tank. If you looked at it another way, it was shaped more like a hooded baby carriage but with searchlights, rabbit ears, a TV set, pressure gauges, sirens, and a strong right elbow jutting out to take the drills, plus who knew what other useful gadgets.

"What is it?" asked Kayak, as he squatted down to have a better look at the strange shapes of the metal snow treads.

"It's Professor Volks' famous Volks Wagon," whispered Charlie. "That's what the international oil men named it. The professor simply calls it Hansel."

"You're looking at the one and only, the smallest, and some say the most unusual oil drill in the world," said Mr. Morgan. "The invention of Professor Wolfgang Volks."

"Holy smoke," said Matthew. "It seems awfully small for an oil drilling rig. It's not like those big ones I saw in Oklahoma."

"If it was any bigger it wouldn't fit inside an airplane," the professor reminded them. "You boys come and help me. I'll show you how the drill arm fits into Hansel's flexible elbow joint. This drill—he patted it affectionately—"I call her Gretel."

With all of them working together they pulled out of the body of the big aircraft endless lengths of magnesium steel piping.

"It's as easy as erecting a Mechano set," the professor said, as he skillfully worked the wrench, fitting one piece to another.

Professor Volks climbed into his beloved Hansel again. "Come on boys, jump aboard and have a ride."

Its snow tracks whirled as it gave them a fast, smooth run along the air strip and circled back again.

"Volkswagen?" Matthew laughed. This Hansel's like a race car."

"What is that?" asked Kayak. "What's a Volkswagen?"

"Lucky you," said the professor. "Imagine, Kayak has never seen a Volkswagen or subway, an *autobahn* or an eight-lane highway, or forty thousand people crushed together at a football game. Kayak has lived a quite different life away from all the cities and crowds. I think, Kayak, that you have lived a truly lovely life without all the smoke and lights and noise."

"Not so lovely," said Kayak. "We heard a terrible lot of noise when a big crowd of walrus chased us across that island. Their roaring was awful."

"Roaring?" shouted Professor Volks. "You want to hear some terrible roaring? You boys listen to Hansel while he turns my new test drills. Nobody north of Patagonia ever heard such a thumping, bumping racket."

"All cargo clear except the dynamite," the Danish

pilot called. "Who's going to take this case of dynamite off my hands? I hate even to touch this stuff."

"I'll take the firecrackers from you, chummy,"
Charlie said. "We used to sleep on dynamite to keep
it cool out on Australia's western desert."

"Don't leave it near the drill site," the pilot warned
them. "Put it far away. Maybe up there on that cliff
away from all the action."

"Relax, chummy," Charlie said. "We'll keep it nice
and cool."

"I'll say cheerio," the pilot called again. "I'm leaving while my engines are still warm, flying back to
Patagonia where it's summer and the trout fishing is
just fine. Have a lovely winter, all of you."

"Sounds mighty good to me," Sergeant Fletcher
shouted, as he pulled up the wolf-trimmed hood of
his blue police parka. "I'd fly down with you, if I
wasn't on duty up here for another year. Right now,"
he said, "I could use a little summer and a change
of scenery." The sergeant pilot smiled and waved his
hand at Kayak. "I'll tell your dad that you're OK—
you take good care of all of them."

Sergeant Fletcher gave a heave on the freight door
and his cheerful red face disappeared as it slammed
closed. The four engines whined into life, creating
their own blizzard of snow that fanned out across
the makeshift airstrip. The huge transport wheeled
around again, the pilot waved. The wide-bodied
plane roared down the lake and took off into the

steel blue sky.

"The thing I like best," said Kayak as he looked around at the jumbled pile of new supplies, "is that yellow towing sled that fits behind the little Hansel."

"That sled is handy," the professor said. "We'll use it later for moving heavy boxes."

"Maybe we can use it right now," Charlie said. "We got to get that dynamite away from here. I'd lift it up with Matilda and put it on that cliff, but we've got to save our gasoline."

"If Mattoosie will help me put it on that new little yellow sled, we can pull it around," said Kayak.

"That's fine," Matt's father said, "but you've got to be careful hauling dynamite. I'll give you both a hand."

He placed a long new coil of strong rope around his shoulders then carefully helped them place the dangerous box of explosives on the sled. Together they hauled the dynamite on the long trip around the rock fault until they came to a place not far from the Number Three drill site. When they looked over the edge of the short cliff, they could easily see the seepage point.

"I can show you a shorter and quicker way to get back to our tents," said Mr. Morgan, and he tied the strong rope around a solid granite rock. "First we'll let down that yellow sled, and then we'll climb down after it."

When the sled touched the ground below, Charlie,

who was waiting there, undid the rope fastenings.

Matt's father said, "I'll go first. You boys watch me carefully, and then follow."

Matt's father placed the rope around his hips and made a special slip knot. "See how that is tied," he said. "You can lower yourself on this."

He turned with his face to the cliff and leaning outwards, stepped off and seemed to walk backwards down the steep gray granite rock face, using the rope as though it were a part of himself.

"*Wahkudlunga!*" said Kayak in surprise. "I want to learn how to do that."

"Who's next?" Matt's father called out to them.

Matthew hesitated, then said in a small voice, "Me?"

"Good!" his father called up to him. "Tie the same double slip hitch that I showed you."

Matthew held his breath as he made the first step backwards. After that, it was not so frightening and he walked haltingly down the cliff face, pushing away from the rock with his feet, sliding a bit, then touching the rock again to steady himself, all the time holding tightly onto the rope.

"*Attai!* Here I come!" shouted Kayak, and he climbed swiftly down.

"Look at him," Matt's father said. "That Kayak is a natural-born mountaineer. He moves like he's been climbing all his life."

As they walked away, Kayak looked back at the

still-dangling rope and said, "Can you go up the same way you go down?"

"Oh, yes," Mr. Morgan nodded. "But it's difficult. It takes more strength. I'll show you both some other time. Now we've got to get to work."

When they had finished dragging the big tarpaulins over their new supplies, they weighed them down with heavy rocks. Ross Morgan and the professor carefully reexamined the crack in the rocks at discovery Number Three where they would begin their drilling. Finally they chose the exact area where the seepage seemed the strongest.

The light new snow was cleared away by Charlie and Kayak, and the professor carefully eased his famous Hansel over the precise spot where they would start the drilling. When the long slim rods were in place, the professor skillfully worked the levers. Matthew saw the drill flash and turn. He heard the slow chewing, grinding, drilling process begin. It was a sound he would hear during every hour for many days to come.

"You'll hear Hansel and Gretel chewing up those rocks even while we sleep," the professor said with pride and patted his noisy miniature machine. "Hansel is just like a mosquito dipping his sucker deeper and deeper, searching for the fossil fuels."

"What you say about Hansel makes it sound alive. My grandmother, she talks like that," said Kayak. "She believes that the stones, harpoons, lamps, everything has got an *inua,* a life, a soul inside it, just like all the animals and the humans."

"Your grandmother may be right," said the professor. "There are many things about this world not yet understood by us."

With the professor directing, everyone worked frantically, as they tried to place each item exactly where it should be on his machine.

"What is this big steel cone for?" asked Matthew as they rolled it over the snow toward site Number Three.

"I don't know," said Charlie. "It looks like a giant fool's cap, the kind we had to wear if we said something bad in school in New South Wales."

"The professor says we should take turns watching the pressure gauges and checking the fuel supply and liquid lubrication," said Matt's father.

"I'll take the first watch," said the professor, "to make sure everything is working smoothly. Then let's go alphabetically. C is for Charlie—one. K is for Kayak—two. M is for Matthew—three. R is for Ross—four. And W is for Wolfgang—five. Everyone take a four hour and forty-eight minute shift and we cover the whole twenty-four hour period. If anything happens," the professor said, "pull this cord and the emergency siren will go *whoops, whoops, whoops!* If you hear that, all come running. Quick!"

The drilling did not all go smoothly and Kayak during his shift had to wake the professor because the yellow machine was going *bump-grind, wack bump-grind, crack bump-grind, thump!* And Mr. Morgan had to wake him because the deep core bit was going *screek-scratch, screek-scratch, eeek!* It badly needed readjusting and a whole bucketful of lubricating oil.

But still, with all their troubles the little yellow Hansel went on drilling, driving Gretel's long thin metal snout deep into the hard bed rock. Down, down she went through the hidden salt domes, penetrating the subterranean basins of Prince Charles Island exploring where no drill had ever searched before.

When Kayak came off his third watch, he said to the professor, "Have you been walking near the drill site in some soft slippers?"

"No," said the professor. "And anyhow I am wearing these big double boots of mine."

"Well, someone has been out there—not a bear." Kayak looked at all their feet. "I don't think it was any one of us."

It was during Matthew's fourth watch in the gray hours of the early dawn that he heard a deep gurgling rumble underneath his feet. He jumped up and ran around the little trembling Hansel, flashing his light. He checked all the gauges. Every one of their needles was pointing to the highest possible pressure and poor Gretel was screeching and her elbow smelled of smoke. Matthew jerked down on the emergency siren signal cord. It set up an unearthly wailing.

He saw the sleeping tent flaps burst open and in the early light Kayak, Matt's father, Charlie and the professor all galloping toward him across the short expanse of snow, still flinging on their outer clothes.

Matthew felt the rocks tremble beneath his feet and suddenly he saw all four runners stop dead in their tracks. He looked behind him just in time to see a huge gush of rich black oil shoot up high above him, flashing, gleaming in the early morning light.

"STRIKE! STRIKE! We've struck it rich!" his father yelled and, grabbing the professor, danced a wild jig with him across the snow.

"Kayamatt is working! Look at those black diamonds flashing in the sky." Mr. Morgan spread his arms and shouted out in joy. "Look what was hiding underneath this island all this time. Matt, Kayak, we've brought in a wildcat. Your Kayamatt is real! It's real!"

"Hold back a moment, please," commanded the professor. "I've got to get my little yellow Hansel out of there right away or he's going to drown in all that hot black oil."

With that, the professor pulled down his ear flaps, clamped on his safety helmet, ran forward, swiftly disengaged the drill collar and climbed into the driving seat of his famous Volks Wagon. He gunned the engine and shifted gears as the geyser of shining oil splattered over him like thick black rain.

Matt saw the little tractor's steel treads grind over some rocks then lurch forward, sending a shower of sparks shooting backwards toward the spouting oil.

"Holy smoke!" Matt's father held his hands before his eyes. "Run! Run for your lives!" he bellowed, as Number Three burst into a roaring, spitting tower of flames.

XIV

DANGER—DYNAMITE!

"RUN! EVERYBODY RUN!" THE PROFESSOR SHOUTED, AS he leaped out of the stalled Hansel and scrambled away in terror from the roaring, spewing flames. Matthew saw the professor duck behind a broken tumble of fallen boulders, trapping himself too close to the hellish, belching firestorm at Number Three well. To save himself Charlie jumped in and crouched down beside the professor.

Matt and Kayak, who were on the other side of the flaming inferno, watched in utter horror as Matt's father staggered through the red glare of billowing black smoke and flame. They saw him stumble over the rough boulders and fall down, trying desperately to protect himself from the killing heat. Now, like

155

Charlie and the professor, he, too, was trapped where no human being could reach him.

The oil fire was increasing, burning with a hideous roaring sound.

"We got to do something fast," yelled Kayak, as he and Matt drew back from the terrible heat.

"How can we get them out of there?" cried Matthew.

"I don't know," yelled Kayak. "We can't go near them. There's too much fire."

"When those big rocks get hot," said Matthew, as he stared in horror at Kayak, "they won't be able to stay . . . alive. We've got to—help them."

"But how are we going to do it? How are we going to get them out?" Kayak asked.

"I'm trying to think," cried Matthew, and in his desperation he turned his back against the searing heat and swirling smoke. "I've heard once . . . yes, I remember! They did it that way in the Alberta oil fields. But I'm afraid that it might kill them. Kayak, it needs lots of dynamite. It's very, very dangerous!"

"We've got to try," screamed Kayak. "We've got to get them out of there. Those rocks are getting hot!"

"Let's go," Matthew shouted, and together they ran the length of the cliff and climbed up onto the top of the rock fault where the dynamite was safely stored.

Matthew very gently lifted the box of explosives in his arms.

"I know of a quick way to get down," Matthew

said. "We can tie this case of dynamite to the rope my father hung and lower it below, then slide down after it."

Kayak nodded and ran after him toward the edge of the cliff.

Suddenly Matt's smooth-soled sealskin boots slipped out from under him. He fell and slithered toward the icy edge, still clinging to the wooden case of dynamite. Kayak lunged after him, and at the very moment when Matt started to go over, caught him by the hem of his parka and hung on like a bulldog. Matthew could feel the fierce heat rising in his face from the flaming well below them.

"I . . . I . . . can't drop it," Matthew groaned. "It will explode and kill us all."

"Hold on tight," cried Kayak, but he could feel himself slowly slipping forward to the icy cliff's edge and he knew that he would never have the strength to drag back Matthew and his deadly box of dynamite.

"Mattoosie," he gasped. "We are going over—together."

"You let go," said Matt.

They started slipping faster.

"Save yourself! Let go!"

At that moment, Kayak felt a pair of powerful hands grip him by the ankles and drag him slowly backwards away from the icy cliff's face. Kayak kept his desperate grip on Matthew's parka and together they were dragged back from the edge.

Matthew closed his eyes and gritted his teeth as he clung with all his might to the lead-heavy box of dynamite.

When they were safe, they could do nothing but lie gasping on the snow, unable even to move their arms after the enormous strain.

"How . . . how did you find the strength," sobbed Matthew, "to drag me back . . . like that?"

"I didn't . . . do it," Kayak whispered in awe. "Someone . . . I don't know who . . . someone pulled me back!"

They both sat up and looked behind them. They saw nothing but the thick black smoke that belched over the cliff face.

"That's impossible," gasped Matthew. "There's no one here but us!"

"I tell you"—Kayak nodded toward the dark curtain of smoke—"we are not alone here! We are not alone!"

Matthew got cautiously onto his hands and knees and crawled until he had a firm hold on the rope. He pulled it back and found that Kayak already had the dynamite strapped to his back.

"You slide down first," said Kayak, "and I'll follow you. Try to break my fall, if I get sliding too fast."

Matthew stood up to go, and as he did, the smoke blew clear and he could see his father below him, stripped to the waist and writhing in pain. His skin glowed red as though he stood before a fiery oven.

"Hold on, Dad," Matthew screamed to his father

and went sliding down so fast that the rope burned
his hands.

He crouched in the awful heat, steadying the rope
for Kayak who came down after him. The flames
lashed toward them, driven by the rising Arctic wind.
They were sprayed with black diamonds of brightly
burning oil that rained down upon them, spattering
across the box of dynamite.

Matthew looked again at the hot jumble of rock
that entombed his father and the place that held
Charlie and the professor. All three seemed to glow
red hot in the fiery light of the flaming oil.

"Follow me!" yelled Matthew.

Kayak ran clumsily after him, feet wide apart, trying not to slip on the snow, which was turning soggy
in the heat, and fall with the deadly dynamite.

When they reached Hansel's small yellow tow
sled, Matthew helped ease the case of explosives
from Kayak's back. Hastily they lashed it to the sled.
Matt tied a long rope line to each front runner. He
handed one to Kayak and took up the other one himself.

Slinging the rope lines over their shoulders, they
started running, pulling the sledload of dynamite behind them. They moved toward the flaming well.

"Spread wide! Spread wide!" Matt shouted, holding up his free hand to shield his face from the terrible heat. "I'll go on one side of the flames. You go
on the outside. SPLIT!" he shouted. "SPLIT WIDE!"

Pulling hard, the two boys spread out, one on each

side of the burning well, to form a long V, with their two pulling ropes coming together at the explosives-laden sled.

"Get ready to run!" Matthew shouted, but Kayak could not hear his words. They were drowned out by the awful roar of the blazing well.

Matthew turned his head. At the end of their long rope V he saw the sledload of dynamite disappear into the base of the towering flames.

"Run, Kayak. Run!" he screamed, as he covered his head and dived for the protection of the nearest rocks.

WHAAAAH WHOOOMPH! The whole case of dynamite exploded in an awesome single blast. It was so close that it made a sound more powerful than any one of them had ever heard before. The earth trembled, then heaved as broken rock rose into the air and rained down all around them.

Matthew cautiously took his hands away from his ears and opened up his eyes and peered again over the hot rock that protected his life. To his amazement he saw that the huge towering flame of burning oil had been blown out like a giant candle by the violent force of the exploding dynamite. A huge ball of black smoke rose into the air.

"It worked! It worked!" Matt shouted to his father. "The old western oilman's trick—it worked. She's finished burning!"

There was no answer, only an awful silence from behind the oil-soaked smoldering rocks.

"Dad! Dad!" Matthew called. His voice echoed in the silence. "Charlie!" he called.

"I'm half-baked," Charlie gasped. "But I'm alive, I guess."

Charlie's singed red hair appeared above the rock. He, too, was stripped naked to the waist.

"I got the professor here with me," he said. "He's still breathing. I think he's just fainted from the heat and shock of that explosion."

"Dad! Dad!" Matthew shouted in desperation, but there was no answer.

Charlie was the first to scramble over the hot rocks in a panic-driven search for his friend. Matthew raced after him, screaming when his hands touched the heated rocks. They found Ross Morgan's body slumped behind a boulder, his skin turned painful lobster red. Together Charlie and Matt dragged his father out.

"He's got to be alive," said Matthew.

"Sure, he's going to be fine, he's tough," said Charlie, and he gently shook Matt's father. "He's like the professor. He's probably just passed out from that awful heat. I tell you, it was terrible in there. It would make the summer desert of Australia seem like wandering in a deep freeze."

Matt's father slowly opened his eyes and looked at both of them and sighed. "Could you spare a pal a little bite of snow to eat," he whispered.

"I watched you through a crack in the rocks," said the professor who was sitting up. "What you and

Kayak did was very, very brave. You saved our lives."

"Kayak! Where's Kayak?" Matthew jumped to his feet.

Kayak was nowhere to be seen. Matthew shouted for him, but there was no answer.

"Here's one of his mitts," Charlie said. "I hate to show it to you because it's scorched black. Looks to me like it was blown right off his hand."

"Kayak! Kayak!" Matthew shouted. "He saved my life up on the cliff. He carried down the dynamite, and now . . . and now . . . he's gone. My brother's gone. Kayak! Kayak!" he screamed.

A voice not far away said, "Not gone, Mattoosie. But pretty near! My parka's blown right off my back."

Over against the cliff wall, with his face scorched and blackened, lay Kayak. Blood oozed from his forehead.

Matthew staggered to him and kneeling, gently wiped his face. "Are you all right?" he asked, as he hauled off his own parka and laid it over Kayak.

"I don't know," Kayak answered in a shaky voice. "I'm afraid to try and move. I'm sure some part of me is going to be broken or torn off."

"Don't move at all until Charlie can help you. Here he comes. He knows first aid."

Charlie wrapped blankets around both of them. "Try your right leg," Charlie said. "That's fine. The left? Goodo! Right arm, left arm. Jolly good. Lift your head a little. Now let's see about the back. Sit up a bit. Fine. You lay back and rest, my hearty. You've had an awful shock. But still, even after all that, everybody's still alive. I'd say we're mighty lucky. Imagine living through all that heat and those big rocks blown up and raining down around us."

Charlie shuddered and pulled on his fire-singed parka. "That damned heat's no sooner g-g-gone than I am shi-shi-shivering cold again."

Professor Volks cried out, "Look at poor Hansel. He is all blistered. He is ruined. And Charlie, look over there. Your helicopter, she is smoking. She's afire!"

"Sweet kicking kangaroos!" yelled Charlie, as he hobbled as fast as he could go toward Matilda.

Her doors hung open from the blast and her seat cushions were ablaze. Charlie flung them out then grabbed Matilda's fire extinguisher and quickly doused the flames. The picture of a kangaroo on skiis painted by Kayak and Matthew was scorched beyond all recognition.

When Charlie tried to rev her engines, her big blades made only one half turn before he shut her off.

"Everybody help me!" the professor yelled. "She's oozing oil! We got to get the steel cap on that well quickly before it has a chance to catch on fire again."

All five of them looking like scarecrows, with sooty faces and burned and tattered clothing, had to use their fire-blistered hands to roll the big fool's cap up to the well head. With a final heave they let it fall in place, covering the still bubbling fountain of hot thick oil that continued to surge out of the rocks.

"Peg it! Peg it down!" the professor shouted, "and I'll pour in the thick coagulate."

When he was finished, they stood back and watched. A little black oil dribbled out around the curved steel collar's edge, and then it stopped.

"She's stiffening! She's capped! She's going to hold!" The professor winced as he hopped up and down waving his blistered hands in the ice cold air.

They went all five together and stood in the burned-out blackened ruins of their big supply tent, which had caught fire from a wind-driven shower of flaming oil.

"Everything in here is useless now," Matthew said.

"My lovely radio's ruined," said the professor sadly. "It's melted, burned to pieces."

Charlie hobbled back to Matilda and pulled out the first aid blanket, which he draped across Ross Morgan's shoulders. "You're a tough old bird with skin like leather," he said to Matthew's father. "Your body doesn't show a blister."

Charlie taped a cut above Mr. Morgan's eye and salved and bandaged both his hands. Next he bandaged Kayak's head. Then he dressed Matt's heat-blistered cheeks and hands, then he took care of the professor's, and finally his own wounds with some help from all of them.

"Friends, I hate to say this after all our good luck

finding ourselves alive and with a brand new oil well. But . . ." Charlie shook his head. "We're still in awful trouble. I'm afraid that poor Matilda's done for. When I tried to start her up, her controls were fused. She won't fly. I . . . I doubt she'll ever fly again."

"Won't fly?" said Matthew grimly.

"And Hansel . . . and our emergency supplies," the professor added, "they're burned up, too. No radio. We can't call to the outside world to send us help."

Charlie and Ross Morgan shook their heads. Matt glanced at Kayak and saw that he was still shivering from shock.

Kayak looked up at the cliff where they had almost fallen and then up at the sky. "We are not alone here," Kayak said. "There are humans on this island watching us."

"That can't be," said Charlie. "You get some rest. You'll feel better in the morning."

Painfully they reinforced the two small tents, which had not burned, against the wind. Matthew, who was helping Kayak cut snow blocks, heard his father say to Charlie, "We found our fortune in black diamonds instead of gold, but what good is oil or gold to us now, if all our gadgets and machines have burned or broken down." As a blast of icy wind struck them he said, "Without food or heat, I wonder how long we can stay alive?"

Even as Ross Morgan spoke, the Arctic wind

gusted up to gale force again. It came howling toward them across the lonely expanses of Prince Charles Island, carrying with it stinging blasts of whirling snow.

"Listen to that, Mattoosie," Kayak called to him. "That's not wolves, or just the wind. That sounds like sled dogs howling. Remember when I told you some-one took me by the ankles and kept both of us from falling with the dynamite? It must have been one of them!"

"Who's them?" asked Matthew.

"I don't know," Kayak answered. "But we wouldn't be alive if they hadn't helped us." He turned and peered into the storm. "I've got the feeling . . . that they are watching us . . . right now!"

"Oh, that can't be," said Matthew. "That was just the wind or a wolf you heard out there."

"We've all been under a terrible strain," said Matthew's father, who had heard what Kayak said. "You're starting to imagine things."

"I wish we had my dog Shulu with us." Kayak sighed. "He could help us, if we try to leave this place."

They crept inside the nylon tents and listened to the violence of the winter blizzard as it smashed and howled against the snow walls that they had built too quickly. Matt's father, the professor and Charlie were huddled in one tent, Kayak and Matt were in the other.

The storm raged over them until the following

morning, then blew away and disappeared as quickly as it had come, leaving behind it silent, bitter cold.

Matthew unzipped the entrance flap and stepped outside their tent. The whole world around them had been wind-sharpened into long, hard snowdrifts.

"Mattoosie, did you see something?" Kayak called from inside the tent. "What is it?"

"It seems to me like magic," Matthew answered.

Kayak leaped outside and he, too, stared in wonder. *"Whakudlunga!"* he said. "Somebody walked right up to our tents early this morning." He squatted down and examined the fresh, heavy tracks of a man. "Mattoosie," he whispered, "you better go . . . wake up your father."

Ross Morgan frowned when he saw the wide footprints and said, "We've got to stay together while we find out who this is."

They followed the human track that led to the brow of the low hill beyond Number One discovery. As soon as they crossed the rise, they saw two newly built igloos, a big raised meat cache, two short sleds and at least a dozen large sled dogs lying near the houses.

"Inuit!" said Kayak with excitement in his voice. "Come on! Let's go down and visit. They'll be glad to help us."

Kayak paused before the larger igloo entrance and coughed politely to let them know inside that he was there. The big dogs stared at them uneasily but kept their distance.

"*Pudluriakpusi*. We have come visiting," he called into the entrance tunnel.

There was no answer.

Charlie walked over to the second igloo and shouted, "Cheerio, folks! Is anybody home in there?"

No answer.

"I'm going in," said Kayak. "Leave the rifle outside and, Mattoosie, you stay close behind me."

He bent down and disappeared inside the low snow tunnel of the first igloo. Everyone followed, and when they stood upright, found themselves inside a round new igloo snow dome that glistened like a million icy diamonds.

More than half the house was taken up with a waist-high sleeping bench made of hard-packed snow. This was covered with two thick white bear hides and a tumble of soft brown caribou skins. A large oval-shaped stone lamp had been carefully set beside the bed. It's long wick burned brightly, fed by a pool of clear seal oil.

"I wonder where they've gone?" said the professor. "They must have been here only a few minutes ago. Do you suppose seeing our red tents frightened them?"

"Oh, no." Kayak laughed. "My people don't get frightened. Maybe they saw a bear or caribou and ran out hunting."

"Why didn't they take this spear or this bow with them?" the professor asked.

Kayak examined both of them with care. "I never

saw anything like these before. The head of this harpoon is chipped flint stone bound to a narwhal's tusk, and this bow is made of bone and strengthened with all these caribou sinews. My people have been hunting with rifles for years," he said. "They don't use things like these. And look at this woman's knife we call an *ulu*. It's the same shape as my mother's steel knife, but this one's made of sharpened stone with a bone handle. This snow knife is made of walrus ivory and it wasn't cut with a saw. It was split. And it has wonderful carvings on the handle. Everything in this igloo," Kayak told them, "is very old. There's not a single white man's thing in this whole house."

They hurried over and looked inside the second house. There was no one there though its lamp burned brightly also. Every tool inside seemed ancient as though it had been made by Stone Age hunters.

When they went outside again, Kayak stared at Matthew in amazement. "I can't believe anything I'm seeing. Those are short dog sleds with bones for crossbars. My grandfather said the Tunik people used to make their sleds like that."

"Who made these igloos? Why do those big dogs seem afraid of us?"

"I really want to see these hunters and their families," Kayak said. "I want to talk to them."

"You won't have to wait long," said Charlie, pointing. "There's one, two, three of them watching us.

Can you see them crouching over there beside the hill?"

Kayak took a few paces toward them, stopped and called out something in his language, *Inuktitut*.

The three fur-clad strangers did not move or answer him in any way.

Kayak walked slowly forward. As a greeting he pulled off his mitts and drew back his parka sleeves in an ancient way his grandfather had shown him to prove he held no hidden knife.

Matthew saw the three strange hunters lay their weapons on the snow and stand, raising their arms in the same way as they moved toward them.

Kayak turned his head and smiled back at his adopted brother. "Mattoosie," Kayak said, "these old-fashioned people coming to us . . . they look like friends to me."

Author's Note

Inukshukshalik on West Baffin Island remains today one of the most remote and mysterious places on earth. This unusual cluster of early human images in stone should be carefully preserved as an historical Inuit site, marking one of man's earlier northern explorations.

J. H.

After serving with the Toronto Scottish Regiment in World War II, James Houston, a Canadian author-artist who now makes his home in Rhode Island and northern British Columbia, lived among the Inuits of the Canadian Arctic for twelve years, nine of them as the first Civil Administrator of West Baffin Island, a territory of 65,000 square miles. His duties as Civil Administrator included acting as explosives officer and mineral claims officer.

James Houston's drawings, engravings and paintings are internationally represented in museums and private collections and appear in numerous books. Among his already published books for young readers are *River Runners, The White Archer, Long Claws* and *Frozen Fire,* the book that first introduces Matthew Morgan and his Inuit friend, Kayak.